When Thinking is the Screaming of the Soul

Or,

A Trudge Through the Infernal Substratum of Common
Experience, as Related by a Trustworthy Co-Traveler
Capable of Death and Holder of the Secret Precepts to
Illuminate the Sphere of Divine Radiance in the
Madness of Wondrous Ha-Ha!

When Thinking is the Screaming of the Soul

Or,
A Trudge Through the Infernal Substratum of Common
Experience, as Related by a Trustworthy Co-Traveler
Capable of Death and Holder of the Secret Precepts to
Illuminate the Sphere of Divine Radiance in the
Madness of Wondrous Ha-Ha!

Discovered by the Blind Madman Phil Jourdan
Daicho Tuan-Chi,
Esteemed Prophet of Tomorrow's Violence,
Attendant to Vajrapani, Master of the Secret,
Exhauster of the Dharmadhatu
And Very Good Boy

PERFECT
EDGE
BOOKS

Winchester, UK
Washington, USA

JOHN HUNT PUBLISHING

First published by Perfect Edge Books, 2020
Perfect Edge Books is an imprint of John Hunt Publishing Ltd., No. 3 East St., Alresford,
Hampshire SO24 9EE, UK
office@jhpbooks.com
www.johnhuntpublishing.com

For distributor details and how to order please visit the 'Ordering' section on our website.

Text copyright: Phil Jourdan 2019

ISBN: 978 1 78904 264 1
978 1 78904 265 8 (ebook)
Library of Congress Control Number: 2019950867

A CIP catalogue record for this book is available from the British Library.

Design: Stuart Davies

UK: Printed and bound by CPI Group (UK) Ltd, Croydon, CR0 4YY
US: Printed and bound by Thomson-Shore, 7300 West Joy Road, Dexter, MI 48130

We operate a distinctive and ethical publishing philosophy in
all areas of our business, from our global network of authors to
production and worldwide distribution.

PRAISE FOR THE AUTHOR

The author is beyond all praise.

A HINT AT CHAPTER ONE

They've been driving in silence for probably more than three minutes now and enough is enough. "Listen, I am, uh," McGeeee says.

Rebecca looks up at him and he can't make her expression out.

"Uh."

"Yeah?"

"I mean listen, we've been driving a long time now and I think we ought to take another break. If that's okay with you?"

"Sure."

"That's alright?"

"Yeah, of course."

"Yeah." McGeeee cocks his head in some direction he intends to mean "nearby" and clears his throat. "Up ahead, there, we can get another coffee."

"That sounds good."

"Sorry to make the trip longer and all. Just seems like a good time for another rest."

They drive in silence some more. He taps his fingers on the wheel a few times. Then stops.

"Right there looks good to me. What you think?"

"That place?" Rebecca doesn't even look.

"Um, yes."

"That's fine, I'm fine with whatever."

"Well but, but if you have a preference. Like if you'd like anything in particular. I don't wanna be making all the decisions."

"What decisions? You're not."

"Okay good. I mean let's just go in there, grab a coffee, I can stretch my legs a few minutes and then we..."

He pulls over. Place looks open, there aren't many people inside, it'll be fine. If he asks her again she'll just say it's fine.

"And then we can hit the road again."

"Okay."

"Alrighty," he says, and gets out of the car.

They go inside. He stands in line. She stands close enough to him to give other people the impression that she, too, is in line. But far enough away that she seems not to like him.

"What'll you have?" he says.

"Oh, nothing for me. I'm fine."

"Oh yeah?"

He looks around, nervous. "On me. Really."

"No no," she says. "Thank you, but there's nothing I need right now."

"Well, uh, look," he says. "It's not about needing. I mean it's fine if you don't want anything, of course, but... I'd be perfectly happy to get you something. You don't have to need it, is what I'm saying. It could be a luxury."

"No thank you, McGeeee. I'm fine."

"Alright, yeah." He clears his throat. Her body is just so tense, she doesn't move, she's like a scarecrow. He can see she's nervous, and yet, she doesn't move, doesn't fidget. It's weird. He's nervous too. Anyone would be nervous around her. But when he's nervous he fidgets. Most people fidget. It's unsettling to see someone go totally still when they're nervous.

He orders a coffee and some sponge cake. The cashier lady looks at him funny, expectantly, then at Rebecca. "Oh, no," he says, "she's fine, doesn't want anything." The cashier lady nods and takes his money.

"Unless I can get you to change your mind?"

"I don't want a coffee, thank you," Rebecca says.

"Wow, hold on a second," McGeeee says. The cashier lady looks back at him. "No no, not you. Sorry." McGeeee turns to Rebecca. "Wait a minute. There's room for uh, for misunderstanding here. I wasn't offering to buy you coffee, like, buying you coffee. Like take you for coffee. That was totally not my intention."

"McGeeee..." Rebecca says. "Really."

"I just wanted that to be clear. I was absolutely not trying to ask you on, like, a quick coffee date. I know this stuff can easily be misunderstood. I don't want to make you feel uncomfortable when we are just working together for the first time."

"I *know*," she says.

"Okay good," he says.

"I'll get us a table," she says.

"Yeah, good idea."

He notices the cashier giving him a dirty look as she hands him his sponge cake. Then she doesn't look at him when she passes him the coffee.

He joins Rebecca at the table.

"Okay, I'll be done with this in like five minutes. Then we can go again."

"Don't rush," she says.

"Nah, I think it's better if we can just get this journey over with. I'm tired."

"The coffee will help," she says.

"Oh yeah, for sure."

"The cake too."

"Sure you don't want some?"

"Yes."

He sips his coffee and lets the silence emerge from the dark gulf between them, as it always does if he doesn't make the effort to keep a conversation going. Fuck it. He's done what he can.

The silence gets uncomfortable fast. But he doesn't say anything. Let her be uncomfortable and tense. He's tried to be pleasant. He tries to down his coffee quickly. It burns his tongue.

"Ow, fuck!"

"What's the matter?"

"Just too... hot. It's okay."

"Did you burn yourself?"

"Yes but it's fine." He wipes his mouth with the back of his hand. "Look, I need to ask."

He didn't know he was going to start with this. But she's giving him that expression again and he's already started, so.

"Look it's just uh, I am aware that there is some kind of discomfort here. And I know I seem to be making it worse."

He's startled her. She's about to say something, but he cuts her off.

"I've clocked on, no problem, loud and clear, that you're not interested in getting to know each other better, but we've been driving for like four hours and we have two more to go, and then we have an entire weekend of working together on a project neither of us seems really all that excited about. So I just need — I know maybe this sounds too intense or something but, but I think it would be a good idea to ask you if I've done anything wrong, or said anything to upset you."

Again she opens her mouth, her head already shaking, but he carries on.

"Because if I have, I would rather know about it and uh, you know, if I am doing anything to upset you and it's going to be a problem, then I think we should be really clear about it so that I can cut it out."

"Jesus, no," she says. "Yes, it's..." She stops, sighs.

"What?"

"Oh my God, it's just..." She sighs again, longer this time. "I don't know what you want me to say. Yeah, it's awkward, it's getting even more awkward, but you, you don't seem to understand that you're..." Trails off.

"What? That I'm what?"

"We're just on a work assignment. We don't have to get personal. I appreciate you trying to make conversation, but the way you're doing it... All this, the way you're..."

McGeeee's heart has either stopped, or started beating so fast he can't feel it anymore.

4

"What do you mean by that?" he says. "What is it?"

"Jesus, I can't believe we..."

"What? Really, please, tell me."

"McGeeee, I don't want to be rude," she begins, and sits up straighter.

"But?"

"But while I do, in fact, have a problem with the way this is going, I don't think it's necessary to, like, lay it all out right here and right now and go into the problem and have some big discussion about it. Like I said, we're just on a work assignment. We don't have to get cozy. Sometimes that can be nice, getting to know the person you're working with, but this — this isn't nice, and I'm sorry about that. But..."

"No but wait a minute," McGeeee says.

"What I'm saying is that we don't need to fix it, and..."

"Yes but hold on. Tell me what the problem is, exactly, so I can cut it out."

She sits up even straighter. "Let me finish what I'm saying and..."

"No but you're not saying what the problem *is*, you're just saying there's a problem. And that doesn't work for me, because I have to spend the rest of this weekend with you."

"Yes."

"And there's a problem, and I'd like to fix. I don't want to be, like, making you uncomfortable for the rest of the weekend. I would feel terrible if that were the case."

"Well the way you're making me uncomfortable," she says, cold and maybe angry, "involves constantly checking in on me to make sure I'm not uncomfortable. So if you just..."

"Wait, hold on a minute," McGeeee says, and puts his hand to his temple and rubs.

"Jesus." She lifts her own hand to her face, then quickly puts it down again. "Look, that's all I'm asking. If you just, please, stop caring whether I'm so fucking comfortable or not, that will help.

Because it's really, really driving me fucking insane. Okay?"

McGeeee stares at her. That same expression is on her face, the unreadable one. But it's anger. That's what it is, it was anger all along.

"Holy shit," he says. "Calm down, will you? There's no need to be hostile."

"I'm not being fucking..." She sighs so loud it just comes across as pure theatre. "Oh man, this is ridiculous. Hostile? Hostile? I didn't want to have this conversation. I don't give a shit, McGeeee. Okay? You insisted on hearing what I had to say, and now you're just... okay, whatever. Whatever. I don't give a shit."

"Well, *Rebecca*, you sure *sound* like you give a shit. And I give a shit. So can't we talk about it properly?"

"Okay, whatever," she says, and stands up. "Finish your coffee, finish your cake, whatever. I'll be outside by the car. Take your time."

"Wait a minute," he says, but she's already walked off.

He plays with his coffee cup. A full minute passes by, more. He can't stare at this stupid table anymore. He stretches, tries to relax, checks out the environment.

A lady, older lady, mid-sixties maybe, from another table, is just... giving him a look. All these people with their damned looks. Why can't they just say what they want?

"What is it?" he asks her.

"You don't have a clue," she says.

"What are you talking about?"

"Whatever happens," she says, gesturing vaguely toward the parking lot, "with her, your situation." She shakes her head. "Whatever happens, you really ought to take a good look at yourself, young man. Because people like you, you're hard to take."

"*Excuse* me? What do you mean by that?"

But she glares down at her book.

"Ma'am?"

"No."

"You started this conversation," he says. He can hear himself, and it doesn't sound good. His voice is straining. "What have you got to do with this?"

She ignores him.

"Fine," he says. He leaves his coffee and his cake and walks out of the coffee shop and back onto the parking lot, where Rebecca is standing with her arms crossed, frozen, her gaze on the ground. She just doesn't move, it's unnatural. She would be so much more relatable, more human, if she would just fidget or move or something. There's no way to read body language like that. Like her body is autistic, it doesn't say anything. He just wants to make it better, make all this better.

"Hey," he says, trying on a calmer tone. In control of himself, of the situation. "Look…"

"Let's just go, please. No more talking."

He unlocks the car. She gets in, buckles her seatbelt, and crosses her arms again.

"Fine," he says.

This time they drive in silence for a good half hour. Man, it's tense. She's tense. From the corner of his eye he tries to check on her, see if she's even breathing. Her chest isn't rising or falling. She just doesn't move, it's ridiculous.

When he finally breaks the silence, he surprises himself. Again, he didn't know he was about to do that.

"On a purely practical note," he says, "we're gonna have to work out a way to cooperate if we're going to meet these people and make a good impression, and get them to feel comfortable around us. They won't let us interview them if we're visibly hating each other from the moment they meet us."

She doesn't answer, doesn't move.

"So uh. You know."

Silence.

"It's important," he says.

"I am talking to them," she says in a monotone. "All you are doing is filming. It's not complicated. We don't have to get along. You just need to get a decent angle, make sure the sound is working, and shut the fuck up, and let me interact with them."

"Yeah, okay," he says, relieved that she's saying anything at all. "But it's more complicated than that."

"No, it isn't."

"Well but it is, because you are super, *super* tense right now, and if you're going to carry that into the meetings, then we're not going to help them open up."

"Yes, McGeeee, I am tense right now. Pointing it out, obviously, doesn't make it better. But I am starting to think you don't get things like that."

"I'm not a moron," he says. He's tapping his fingers on the wheel again. The sound is probably irritating her, so he stops.

"No, you're not a moron."

"So don't talk to me like one."

Another sigh from her. "I am extremely baffled right now, and tired, and I don't feel capable of having any more conversations. Clearly this is going to be a tough weekend. We are going to have to get through it because we're professionals. All you need to do is film me talking to them. All I have to do is talk to them, get them talking, let you film them talking, and ask some questions. And then on Sunday morning we'll do the same thing again with the other family, and then we'll have some nice easy footage for the other people at work to pick and choose from and do whatever they want with. Then on Sunday afternoon we drive back and that's it. No more. That sounds relatively simple to me, and it can stay simple."

"Why are you talking to me like I'm a child?"

"I'm not talking to you like you're a child."

"Then what the hell is that tone for?"

"Okay, fuck this. Pull over at the next town, I don't care what

8

it is."

"Are you kidding me?"

"I'm not kidding. This isn't worth it."

McGeeee slows the car down enough to give her a long and incredulous stare. "Are you kidding me?"

"I am not kidding. I'll take a bus back, I don't care. You are, seriously, the most unbelievable, unbearable person I've ever had to work with, and I don't need this."

"No fucking way."

"Excuse me?" It's amazing how she can talk like that and still keep her whole body basically motionless.

"I'm not stopping at some random town and abandoning you."

"Aband— Are you... out... of?"

"Exactly how would that go down at work, huh? I call McDurrrr and I tell him you just threw in the towel and decided to go home and left me to interview these people by myself?"

"You can tell McDurrrr whatever you want. I'll tell him what I have to say too."

"Well holy fuck, why don't you just tell *me,* huh? Why don't you just grow up and tell *me* what your deal is?"

"I have told you my deal and I want you to pull over. Now. Pull the fuck over."

"You're being so unreasonable," he says. "It's just impossible to make any sense out of it."

"Pull over, please."

"I'm not going to pull over on the highway. Stop being ridiculous."

"I swear, if you don't pull over..."

"I can't pull over while we are driving on the highway, you understand? Look, I'm sorry for whatever I did or said. I'm just totally confused now. But I'm sorry."

"Go fuck yourself."

"I said, *I am sorry.* Okay? I'm sorry. I did not, *I truly did not mean to upset you."*

"Shut the fuck up!" She's definitely at screaming level now.

"You know what?" McGeeee says, finding it easier to be calm now. "McDurrrr told me you could be, like, intense, but he did not warn me it would be like this."

"What..." She goes silent.

They drive for a while. He doesn't dare press on now. Another one of those moments he didn't know he was about to bring on, another thing he wasn't aware he was about to say.

"McDurrrr what?" she says, real quiet now.

"Nothing. It doesn't matter."

"What did McDurrrr say?"

"Rebecca, it doesn't matter. He didn't say anything."

"McDurrrr *warned* you that I could be intense?"

"No, no, not like that. Fuck. You're completely misunderstanding this."

"Enlighten me, you condescending son of a bitch."

"Hey, what the hell? We're going to call each other names now? That's how this is going to get resolved?"

"McDurrrr has no business saying shit like that to people who haven't met me. And to talk about me like I'm...like he needs to warn people about me, it..."

"Oh come on. You're not getting it."

"McDurrrr tells you I'm intense, and you prepare yourself for an intense bitch, is that it? And then whatever I do, it's because I'm intense. I get it now."

"Nobody called you a bitch. Be reasonable, for God's sake."

"This is eye-opening, thank you, McGeeee."

"I can't believe you're that upset about something that you clearly don't even understand, it's just insane."

"Yeah, there it is. Intense, insane. And now you're gonna talk to McDurrrr and, yeah, I can picture it already. 'I did everything I could to make her feel comfortable, I tried to make small talk, I offered to buy her a coffee a couple of times. She just wasn't having it. She just couldn't hold up a basic conversation. We stopped for a coffee a second time, and I asked her if she wanted anything, but she was just being so cold, so, so intense and unsociable I tried to make it clear I wasn't asking her out, just wanted us to be able to work together, but she's just like you said, an intense woman. Didn't even bother trying. And then when I tried to figure out what was going on, she..."'

"Come the hell *on*," he says.

"'She just said I was making her uncomfortable but wouldn't say why, and stormed out of the coffee shop. Really. It's crazy. Then we drove on and she just sat there all moody. And when I tried to point out that if we were gonna do our job, we'd have to strive for a basic level of cooperation, she freaked out and told me to pull over and...'"

"Seriously, you are not getting this."

"'And she just suddenly couldn't bear the idea of doing what we'd gone out there to do, and said she didn't care about it, and she'd just take a bus home. I know! I have no idea what the hell her deal is.'"

"You've got it totally wrong. I hate to say it, but you're just flat-out overreacting."

"Yes, exactly. And you're so blind you don't see what you're doing."

"What am I doing?" he says, and notices his voice straining again.

"You're just one of those people, aren't you?"

"What? What are you saying?"

"You're just one of those people who never really do anything wrong, so you can never pin them down, because they're just so fucking disconnected from their own bullshit, so clueless about their contribution to the mess they keep finding themselves in that they manage to get away with it."

"Come the fuck on, Rebecca, what is this?"

"People like you, you don't even qualify as insane, because

you're not insane, you're never actually doing anything *wrong*, you're just trapping people. You lay out traps for people and you don't even know it, and they, they fall into those traps because nobody expects to have to deal with people like you."

"People like me? People like...why don't you just shut the fuck up, huh?" McGeeee's voice is back to deep, masculine, confident. She's clearly out of her mind, but he's damned if he's going to let her carry on assaulting him like this.

"Why don't you just pull the fuck over and we can be done with this? Fuck you and fuck McDurrrr and this fucking job. I've had to learn the hard way that it's not worth sticking in a job where someone like you exists. I feel sorry for whoever's had to work with you on a regular basis. It just doesn't work. You never do anything wrong."

"What is your obsession with me doing something wrong? You're obsessed with that. What is your problem?"

"Yeah, exactly. It's all my fucking problem. Pull over. I know people like you. I've suffered enough because of people like you. You're just unplugged from yourself. Not worth it. Not fucking worth it. Pull over."

"It is literally insane to pull over here."

"Pull over."

"Calm the fuck down."

"Pull over!" she screams, and grabs the wheel.

He smacks her arm away.

"What are you *doing*, you crazy cunt?"

She freezes again, and closes her eyes.

"You're going to kill us both, you know that?"

"Don't call me a cunt. You understand? Don't call me insane, or intense, or anything at all. Just please, McGeeee, I am begging you now. It is perfectly possible for you to pull over. There is nobody ahead of us or behind us. Please, please pull over and let me out."

"And what, you're just going to hitchhike your way back?"

"Whatever, it doesn't matter. Please."

"I would never forgive myself, or be forgiven by anyone else, including our boss, do you understand? It is the wrong thing to do. This has nothing to do with you or with me, it's just fucking reasonable and logical not to pull over. It is really, really dangerous. You could fail to hitch a ride. You could be walking for miles and miles alone and vulnerable. You could get raped."

"Oh my God," she says, almost laughing now.

"You think that's funny?"

"You're a master at this."

"A master at *what*, Rebecca? Huh?"

"At destroying people with your obliviousness."

"Okay, yeah, sure. Insult me all you want, but I am not leaving you on the side of the road. It's not happening. It's just fucking ridiculous."

She slams her palm onto his steering wheel.

"What the..."

"Pull! This! Fucking! Car over right the fuck now, you son of a bitch!"

She hits the wheel again, then hits him.

"You're gonna fucking kill us!" he screams.

"Fine!" she screams back, and carries on hitting him.

"You know very well I can't hit you back," he says. "You're taking advantage of that."

"Pull over!"

"Fuck you."

"Pull over! Jesus, please, please pull over!"

She's gripping the wheel now. He crushes the brakes, swerves to the side and off the road.

Time slows. There's something in front of the car. He sees it all happening, the car elegantly sliding toward the signpost. It's just a signpost, he thinks. Thank God, oh man, they're just hitting some signpost.

There is no such thing as time anymore. They enter something like a zero-space, strangely safe, null, a place to die. He feels the car hit the signpost, sees and hears the airbags spilling out and filling up like, like majestic animals of some kind, swans opening out their wings maybe. He feels a thrill in his spine, blissful contact of forehead and airbag. His foot is still on the brake. The engine's making a sound. The car isn't moving anymore. There's a whirring somewhere. He swims like this, floats in it.

When he comes to, he looks over at Rebecca. Her face. Her face is covered in blood. He can tell, even though he can't see it. She's buried her face in the airbag, which appears to be, what, deflating now. She's not moving.

"Are you..." he says. "Hey. Are you okay?"

She doesn't move, doesn't make a sound.

"Jesus," he says. "Rebecca."

He reaches out and shakes her.

"Hey. Tell me you're okay."

There's a kind of whirring sound, there's a deflating sound. He's shaking her.

"We hit a signpost," he says. "It's okay. Just a signpost. We got very fucking lucky."

He's still shaking her.

"Could have been a wall. Or another car."

Shaking her.

"Talk to me."

He can't believe their luck. Just a signpost. Thank God. It could have been much, much worse.

"Rebecca, come on. Talk to me. Are you okay?"

AN ALTERNATIVE TO CHAPTER ONE, PLEASE SELECT YOUR FAVORITE

After two months they agreed to clear out the room. Rebecca stayed out with a friend that morning and McGeeee carried the crib down into the garage, then the little cushions, the various items not to be used, not yet, everything packed into a neat corner in the garage, neater than the things around it, as though at any moment he might return to fetch the crib again and set up camp.

Now the room was empty, light blue, sunlit, excessive in the new arrangement. It could be an office. She could use it to do something. "Do what?" she'd say. "What can I possibly do with that room? Why should I have to do anything with it? Why me?"

"You don't have to do anything with it," McGeeee would say. "I was only suggesting."

"Suggesting what? That we stay practical? Was this part of the whole thing? A plan? First you get the room cleared out. Time to move the old girl on, you think, best to get her used to seeing it empty right? Then the room's a waste. We'll have to do something with it, maybe you can suggest something to her, maybe she can use it as an office."

"You're being unfair," he'd say, and now he's closed the door to the room and sat on the living room sofa, staring at it, at the door, defending himself. "You think I'm trying to be practical because I'm…because I enjoy it, or I don't have a heart? You think it brings me pleasure to force you to confront what's in our house, what's in our lives, this loss?"

She'd start mumbling something, but his mind had already carried on. "You think my only duty as your husband is to sit around feeling the exact same sorrow you feel, in the exact same way, that when I stray from the one path of true sorrow you set out for us it's because I don't take you seriously, I don't take what's happened seriously, I don't...I'm not capable of loving what we lost? We lost the same thing and we need to lose it the very same way? And if I refuse to mourn the way you mourn it's a form of rebellion?"

And how she'd turn to him: the look of suffering, her look of suffering, unique to moments of...what could he call her without insulting her? Convenient moments. Moments to let the pain show, to still the flow of things, make him focus on what he was doing to her, how what he said did not sit well with her, how he owed her an apology. And would not grant it because to him the very idea of granting an apology was not a problem, because, as she'd said, hadn't she, he always felt that apologies must be earned, that an empty apology was ridiculous, without purpose, even destructive. Didn't he?

"I don't have to apologize for...for not apologizing whenever it..."

She could quiet him even in his daydreams. She could look at him with that face of indignant suffering, like a boy sent off to war looking back to say: The folly of what you're doing.

"But I don't have to apologize for not suffering like you. I don't have to. I never will. How can you pretend to love me when...when the very thing that you seem to love is my refusal, my decision never to pander to people who..." only to trail off into real, spoken words, spoken at the air around him, mumbled at first: "...always said what you loved in me was that I didn't feel the need to apologize for things that warranted no apology, always said it, don't say it now perhaps, now it's real and involves you," then louder, and he stood to pace and spoke as though she were in the room with him. "Now it makes you feel inadequate, that I don't cry as soon as you do, that I don't violate the right taboos, that I could even dare to think to myself that maybe this..."

"This what? This whole what?"

"I didn't say this whole anything. I..."

16

He opened the door again and stood where the crib had been. Then lay flat on his back and stared up at the ceiling to see what the baby would have known for those long months of crying staring up waving his little hands impotently to clutch at things. The ceiling had been painted over months before. Everything redone, the wallpaper light blue because we are expecting a boy and my aunt who was a midwife said you need to show babies the right colors early so they understand…

"Understand what, God damn it, understand they're boys or girls? Understand the…you think keeping a newborn boy in a pink room is going to make him gay?"

And she'd say, correctly, that they'd been through this, that it had nothing to do with the baby ending up gay. Why did he always need to make her sound like a homophobe?

"Because you…because your damned crazy aunt who also thinks you should tip seven percent exactly every time, bring a calculator if you need to, because of some crazy tax loophole, she thinks it helps the waiter if…I mean the woman's an idiot, she's ignorant to the point of criminality, thinks you can call the police when the milkman kept her waiting too long, and you listen to her about this insanity, that babies need gender reinforcement from day one? You listen? You think she's the kind of woman I want telling us how to raise our children?"

"Raise our…what is the problem? She's not raising our children, we have no…" and the face of suffering again, the plunge into sobbing for him to take note and remember she was fragile.

"I know you're fragile, damn it. I know. But can't you see the madness of…I mean your aunt's a monster. And I worry about it. I worry that…"

"She isn't a monster. Why must you insult her?"

"I worry that she'd have tried to interfere. That she'd have invited herself over with her crazy big rings and her crap about sunlight causing more cancer in babies who lacked this or that vitamin, that she'd have come in here and said this must go and that must go. Change this. Tell your so-called husband to do it for you. That she'd have butted in every chance she got and..."

"She wouldn't have. And she won't."

An obvious silence to ensue, gigantic, like a rubber band they would stretch out as long as possible by moving away from each other until it snapped and he...what? As though his pain were simply not good enough, did she want him to sit around howling at her side saying I cannot go on, I cannot endure? "You use these moments like weapons. You think these silences need to be observed, their meaning must be respected. That if I don't wallow in them the way you do I must clearly not care at all that our child is dead, was born and died, was dead out of you? That you were there with him one minute and alone the next and looked at me with those eyes I could barely..."

McGeeee stood and closed the door again, sat back on the sofa. She must be sitting in the light out in a park somewhere, perhaps complaining about him, his coldness. And her friend — which friend? — nodding in disappointed assent, mhm-hmm I always suspected he wasn't good with feelings. The cold, indifferent, repressed husband. Tries to get everything out by changing the physical things, keeping busy, clearing out the baby's damned room straight away.

"Straight away? Two months. Two months, the thing wasn't even...the baby wasn't...we never got our baby. We never got him home. I never put him in that crib, damn you. I never saw him in that room, he never saw the blue wallpaper, your crazy aunt never came around to fix our parenting, don't you...two months of what? Of you. Of you sitting around wanting me to suffer just like you. Of me not being allowed to suffer any other way. If I don't cry it's because I don't care. If I don't...we never got him here, damn you. He never existed here except as preparation, as us just talking and talking about him. He was always something we needed to think about very carefully, to plan for, to make room for, to worry about, to warn employers about. He was change. He was evolution. I was going to learn to be less selfish, wasn't I? Wasn't he going to change my entire perception of the world? He was a...he could fix us, could make you want me around and make me want to be around, isn't that part of it? Wasn't that lurking there for you? That at least we'd... that I could at least have a reason not to get out of here and give up, that whatever we had that was good might be improved by our bonding over this false hope of family and...am I the only one? Can you possibly sit there staring at me like what I'm saying is wrong, that it surprises you? I mean, God, it's...he was..."

The phone rang. The silence had been total. The city outside returned with the ringing: the talking outside, birdsong. The sunlight was the coldest thing on his body. He picked up the phone. "Yes, darling. Yes, I'm...I'm glad. Is she there with you still? Oh, I...yes. Can you ask her if...no, that's fine. I'll come get you right away. Of course we can. Yes, I...I did. It's...it's very empty. It's made me very sad, I think. I think maybe we shouldn't let you look inside right away. It's just so empty and somehow quieter than it was. Okay, that's... Yes, I'll take the car right now. Why don't you wait inside, where it's cooler. Love you, too, I'll see you soon. Okay. Love you too."

And looked for the keys.

19

A THEMATIC EPILOGUE,

UNRELATED TO WHAT HAPPENED IN CHAPTER ONE BUT, IF TAKEN IN THE RIGHT WAY, SERVING AS A GLIMPSE INTO THE MADNESS OF THE AUTHOR

People were always surprised to discover that McGeeee wasn't as short as they remembered. He knew this, the way short men know they are short even when no one is watching. He wasn't even short, anyway, and he never thought about it in those words; but he had always sensed, in the looks others gave him when they were not quite sure who he was, that failure to take him seriously, as though he had mustard on the side of his face. Something about McGeeee. There had always been something. That visible, overflowing eagerness in his body to press down on things he could not control; his odd, undeclared struggle to be in charge of his own body. That was what most gave him away. He could not *live* in his own body, and this gave him an agitated, buzzing, over-calculated presence that others simply registered as the overcompensating energy of a short man. But he wasn't even short.

He had given up eating lunch with his colleagues because he sensed their sense of his shortness. The mood, the gestures in the office always changed at lunch time, when people rolled their sleeves a bit further up and loosened their ties and began exaggerating the symptoms of stiff backs, stretching out their arms a little wider, speaking a little louder about things of no relation to work. Then, usually between noon and ten past noon, the lunch hour was officially announced by the boss, who was actually short and — according to a secretary who no longer worked there — mostly impotent. At that point, everyone stopped work and ate something somewhere. Most men in the

20

office broke up into small groups and disappeared to one of the restaurants nearby, where they flirted with waitresses, told jokes they'd told before and complained about the state of the industry. McGeeee had once been one of these men, had briefly belonged to one or another of those groups, but less than a year into the job, he'd decided to eat at his desk, and had eaten at his desk ever since.

"What's the matter, Pat?" one of his former lunch partners, Geoff, said, on the first day of McGeeee's new life as the office loner. "Get up, we're going."

But McGeeee — who had never asked to be called Pat — took out a cling-wrapped cheese and tuna sandwich he'd packed at home from his jacket pocket, placed it on his table, and looked up. The sandwich was perfectly square, expertly boring. "I'm not going today. I have to finish something."

"Finish what?" Geoff said.

McGeeee pointed at his table.

"You brought a sandwich?" Geoff yelled. "Mart, hold on a second. Our pal Pat brought a goddam *sandwich* for lunch."

"He what?" Mart said from the reception.

Others were staring.

"I just need to finish my work," McGeeee said. "I'll see you later."

"Brought a sandwich," Geoff said, gesturing at McGeeee so McDurrrr, who had just emerged from the toilet, could know. But there was no more discussion, and McGeeee ate his sandwich and tried his hand at his first crossword puzzle in a decade.

Years passed, about three. He noticed, from that first day of his quiet revolution, that nobody ever asked him out to lunch again. It had only taken one act of defiance. And did you see? That was no simple insult, but a complex confirmation of all he feared. He had no conceptual understanding of anxiety — he called it being on edge, if he called it anything at all, something he could drink away or distract himself out of by taking up new hobbies he never maintained — but his anxiety grew every morning from that first day on; for now he could not bear to join anyone for lunch, but dreaded, resented, not being invited. He felt it in his chest, a tension in his back and a wetness in his armpits, the minute he woke up, without pause, until the minute he tricked himself into falling asleep somehow.

Three years of not quite belonging, of his failure to belong not quite mattering in the grand scheme, of being taken for small, of crafting for himself a reputation of not being a bad guy but you know, a bit on the weird side. A bit on the fringe, they must think.

They must think worse of him than they dared speak of him. He suspected this, entertained the fantasy of being described as really, really not a bad guy, but a bit weird, just not a *bad* guy. What could they possibly say, except that they knew little of him? Nobody could feign a better knowledge of him than they had, because he so visibly spoke to no one. He turned up and did his job and ate at his desk and yes, maybe at some point he'd been a bit more sociable, but back then Mart Hellmann and Alex Bull were still working there and now they weren't. And there was still McDurrrr but he wouldn't say much about anyone, thought gossip was for women who couldn't get pregnant anymore and said so. People didn't last long at that office, but McGeeee had lasted, and okay, he was a bit weird, but he was an old-timer. Maybe he was sick of fraternizing. You could say nothing truly awful about McGeeee, and he knew it; you could think what you wanted to think, but he wasn't a bad guy, and nobody could disagree with that. He imagined the cocky new intern cracking some joke about weird, quiet McGeeee; something about the new hair, because McGeeee hated what the stylist had tried to do, and assumed everyone must be looking in silent shock. He imagined the intern saying the hair looked like a taxidermist had tried to stuff a Pomeranian using little dead hedgehogs; and he imagined someone, maybe the quiet young Polish man who had been there about a year, a friendly face, saying, "Hey now, yes, the hair is weird, but McGeeee is a good guy. He's just quiet, he's mysterious, that's all." Yes, he was weird — well, not weird, no, just quirky, and not a bad guy. And the intern, after protesting and seeing in the expressions of his listeners that he ought not to protest, finally gave in, and McGeeee numbly delighted in having his reputation protected by someone he didn't even know, in the presence of others, who, if they were ever in any doubt, would now know that Other People were fond of McGeeee.

One morning, about two years after his first sandwich at his desk, McGeeee had woken up from a deep sleep, totally free: blissfully present. Just there, not even there, just.

It had gone on for just a couple of hours: the sensation, physical and emotional and perhaps spiritual, of being utterly unhindered, at liberty to be in the world just as he wished, enlightened, made lighter. He noticed this as soon as he woke up: a curious lightness in his fingertips. His blanket felt like an ongoing caress. His eyes were wide open and took in every crack in every surface of every thing. The light revealed details. Details! He could see details in things without trying: the wrinkles in his pillow were as deep and intricately created as the whole of his inner life. None of that habitual dread of getting out of bed and into clothes and into the foreign land of being himself — nothing of the kind. Nothing was wrong that morning; nothing worried him, no one angered him.

He couldn't believe it, and spent the first hour of that day amazed that even his failure to believe it was all happening couldn't stop it from happening. He felt good *no matter what*, relieved to be alive and not dead, but perfectly happy to die someday, even today, if that must happen. He looked forward to death because he knew for certain there was no death, and knew the place of death in life, knew the absolute necessity of the end. And likewise he saw — saw directly, with his own eyes — the inevitability of life. Life was more than beautiful: it was unstoppable, so enormous, so powerful it could not even contain its own power, and death was simply a space into which life, in its excess, overflowed. But death was also that part of life which made life so full and plentiful in the first place; and if the hypothetical finitude of death were not there taking up so much space, life would not overflow into death. It was no paradox.

"Yes!" he said, as he prepared for work. "Yes, yes, yes. Yes to all of this, God damn it!"

He knew the secret to bliss was to stop looking for secrets, and as he stepped onto the train that morning he knew he had stopped the quest of secrets entirely. He saw in everyone a shard of that great cosmic stupidity from which all souls had come. The whirring of the train was exactly right. The train was delayed, and it was no problem: there were no true delays, there was no rush, the only necessity was the necessity of things as they were, and McGeeee, whose very name was a meaningless formality representing nothing, was witness to all of it.

"Good morning!" he said when he arrived at the office. He had said it to no one in particular, so everyone looked up. And he had meant it, for it was a good morning, and he wished everyone could see how good that morning truly was, not just for him, but for everyone. He had been filled overnight with love for every person in that office, for every person he'd passed on the street to get there. But suddenly something shifted underground, or in him: someone mumbled, "Good morning," without looking up; someone else said something that didn't even sound like a word. Others were already burying their faces in their own mornings again. And McGeeee unceremoniously lost what he'd found.

Everything slowly folded back into everyday unhappiness.

He spent a long time sitting at his desk with a pen in his mouth. The tension in his muscles had returned. All around him the faces of colleagues flickered on and off as he tried to blink himself back into that peace. Nothing. The easeful bliss was gone, though it had not been entirely replaced by the usual misery all at once. Instead he felt the quality of his experience gradually changing back into the familiar horror, with the same discomfort one feels when listening to a child winding a music box without any sense of the timing of a familiar tune.

And as lunchtime approached, McGeeee noticed a particular theme creeping back into his thoughts. Little by little he had begun to feel small again. Tiny McGeeee. His body had shriveled up again, and for the first time he was fully aware of how uninspiring and pathetic his posture tended to be: his hunched shoulders, his fists like the tight pistachios you throw away. That was it, what had been missing in the morning: his usual sense of smallness. He had had a taste of life without littleness, and he'd had it in his own body. So it was possible to be free right where he was! Freedom within his own life, his own ugly, tense body, was no lie. It was real and could be found. And although he had been set aflame by the obviousness of everything during his foray into freedom that morning, he never would have understood the role that his feeling of smallness truly played in his ordinary misery if he had not been jolted out of that freedom. Perhaps, then, even the loss of the gift had been a part of that gift.

He hoped, half-consciously, that this latter realization would restore the bliss; it did not. And someone's hand gripped McGeeee's shoulder.

"Could you come into my office, please?" It was his boss, Evans, looking down at him with an expression of either sadness or perplexity.

McGeeee followed, and was conscious of his shoulders hunching even more as he walked.

In his boss's office, McGeeee moved to a chair and started sitting down, and Evans just managed to say, "Please sit down" in time to make it seem that McGeeee was following his orders.

"You're looking distracted," Evans said.

"Um," McGeeee said.

"Everything okay?"

"Oh, yes. Just a strange morning, sir."

"Mornings are always strange. Waking up isn't natural." Evans pretended to shuffle some papers on his desk. "Listen, McGeeee. I'm retiring."

"Oh, wow, sir."

"Yes, wow. I'm done. I can afford to retire early and I'm going to retire early. I am getting the fuck out of here as soon as possible."

"Congratulations."

"Yes, well. Would you be willing to take over?"

McGeeee blinked.

"Huh?"

"Replace me."

"Me?"

"Why not? I know people underestimate you, but I also know I don't underestimate you. You understand? You're good at all this. You could do with learning some people skills, sure. That's secondary, though. This whole setup we have here, all of us, it's all down to letting people carry on, doing their thing without too much management. It's been an interesting experiment for me, you know, seeing how little actual managing I could get away with and still get results. That's the way things should be. Don't over-manage, just let people do what they are good enough at doing that you pay them to do it, see."

"But..."

"Now hold on, I'm not done. I want you to consider taking over this desk. Be the man people go to if they have questions, but don't manage people. Every attempt at management risks becoming over-management. Anyone else in this building, they'd over-manage. Only you have the knowledge and the lack of interest in people that I consider sufficient for effective non-management."

Then Evans gave McGeeee the first five seconds of full eye contact McGeeee had ever received from anyone.

McGeeee cleared his throat. "God, but..."

"More money, less work, McGeeee. You are grossly undervalued here. Some might even say you enjoy being undervalued. Time to reward you for your particular brand of isolation and competence."

At that moment, McGeeee realized — but how? — that if he could just hold his mind a certain way, he would be plunged back into the limitless freedom from earlier that morning. Something within had shifted, had *understood* something else. That freedom, that beauty, could be summoned back.

Evans was clicking his pen and making an impatient breathing sound.

McGeeee wanted only to turn his mind back to the ocean of freedom that resided somewhere in the realm of unceasing possibility. Please. But he was just short, undervalued McGeeee. Isolated and competent McGeeee.

Before he could respond, he noticed himself saying, "No thank you, sir."

Evans was as taken aback as McGeeee was.

"Oh, come on."

"I just can't," McGeeee said, again without his own consent. As though he'd split off from his own miserable tiny self, but instead of joining the cosmic grandeur, he'd merely been stapled onto that tiny self as an even tinier, more miserable, passively observing self. The smallest conceivable McGeeee, helplessly watching a mechanical, terrified, resentful everyday McGeeee turning down a promotion.

"Let's at least talk about it, see if I can change your mind," Evans began."

"No, sir, thank you," Robot-McGeeee said. "I enjoy my job just as it is."

"And you wouldn't enjoy it more in your own office? More

solitary that way."

"No, sir." But he would, he would certainly like his own office, with a door, with silence.

"Take a day to think about it."

"No, sir."

"Oh, fuck you, McGeeee," Evans said, almost good-naturedly, as though none of this was in any way surprising to him.

As he walked back to his desk, McGeeee felt the world shrink around him. Worse, he shrank with it.

A year later, McGeeee had not forgotten his experience of absolute liberation that one morning, but he'd given up trying to replicate it. The whole thing had been like a dream, and like any dream that has been interpreted to death, it no longer felt like something relevant to him. Perhaps he'd just had a psychotic break. Or maybe he had some kind of chronic sleep problem that he'd never been aware of, an inability to get the kind of rest that others took for granted, and that magical morning had been the result of his first good night's sleep. Maybe that was just how anyone who slept properly felt when they got out of bed. Could it be?

till, the memory nagged at him. He'd give anything to know that openness again.

And, one Sunday morning, he did. Sleep was good. Was deep. As soon as he'd opened his eyes, he knew the mysterious shift into freedom had occurred again. The vividness was back — the lucidity — the flow of movement within all solid objects — the spaciousness — the pulsating stupidity and beauty and intelligence of what was right in front of him. Here it all was again. The ceiling was made of light. The light was made of silence. Moving out of bed was like a shapeless dance, a silk

28

ribbon unfurling upward into space, an egg falling into a tub of jelly. Language was slipping away. McGeeee was gone but the room remained, though not as a room, for clearly all of the world could be collapsed into an ebbing flowing

The body of the person moving toward the window, which wasn't even a window, to look out into the street, to see, to be gushing, gush out of the eyes, to spill out into this and take it as real and good and here, if even that, laughing, just big belly laughing belly out, belly in, out until the world was forced to know that this

all of this was very good and null belly laughing! Belly laugh in out, in out, banging on the walls, laughing through the window so the street would know

see through one thing and all is seen through!

wu-huuuuu

THE SUCCUBUS FROM LATER ON

Rebecca, dreaming, was on the roof. She had only stepped out for a quick cigarette, but now that she was up here, she really didn't want to go back down again. It was okay to take a few minutes and compose herself.

Not that there was anything wrong. She wasn't sure why she needed a time out. Just one of those things. Sometimes the body knows, as her mother had often said. You can trust the body to tell you when it needs a break. All you have to do is learn to listen. But anyway, Rebecca wasn't sure she needed a break. She just didn't want to go back down.

People were being loud down there. She had thought she was coming to a simple gathering of friends, but it had become boisterous quickly and unexpectedly. People she had never met were turning up, and introducing their friends to other people's friends, and the mood had changed into something Rebecca didn't know how to deal with. She had never learned how to do this kind of thing, how to look nonchalant when meeting people she found threatening. She wasn't even sure why she found them threatening. But she did. Her body told her so. A couple of guys in particular had made her unbearably uncomfortable without saying anything. There was just something about them, about the way they looked at each other before saying hello to her. She didn't know how to interpret that.

But then, she knew that if she had decided to stay at home, she would probably be asleep by now. She had promised herself to make an effort and to be sociable and show her face once in a while. Maybe she just needed to learn how to deal with these situations. She had read in an article somewhere that the body responds to danger way before the mind has any idea that there is something wrong. Something to do with hormones, she remembered, and the lizard brain. So, the article had said, one way to learn how to cope with social anxiety was to place yourself in uncomfortable situations repeatedly, to let the body know it was perfectly possible to survive the initial terror. Gradually, the body would relax in previously scary social environments. When she had read this article, Rebecca had made the resolution: no more hiding from life. She had no right to complain about being lonely if she didn't make an effort to meet people. She would go out of her way to engage in conversations and make more friends. At least, that had been the intention.

And yet here she was, smoking a cigarette on the roof of somebody's house. She had gone through the window of a bedroom, as she had seen so many other people do that evening. She had told herself that this was edgy behavior, that this was a way to confront her fears. She had never done this before; she hadn't been one of those people who smoked on roofs and looked out into the night. So this was progress. Except that she had waited until there was nobody else out smoking, had hung around occasionally glancing at the roof to see if anyone was still there. Then she had gone out by herself, and moved to the farthest corner of the roof, where it looked safe. She had spent the last ten minutes hoping nobody would join her.

So, she knew this didn't count as progress.

"BITCHES!" someone screamed from below.

"I am the High Priest of the nothing-bubble!" another replied.

"Suck a dick, bitches!"

"Tequila!"

How did these people do it? How did they simply turn up, shake hands or kiss each other, exchange a few words of greeting to those they'd never met before, and then seamlessly create the illusion that they were all friends already, that there was a point in the past at which they had already bonded? How did people know how to carry themselves so that others would assume there was no fear, no neediness and no desperation? Then again, maybe things were even simpler than that. Maybe there really was no fear or neediness or desperation. She had spent her whole life assuming people were primarily actors, playing a role that wasn't necessarily comfortable for them, because that was just how you did the social life thing. She had always taken the nature of social interaction to be bad theatre. Other people were just better actors than her. But what if they were actually enjoying themselves down there? It struck her now that she had never truly considered this option.

Anyway, she shouldn't ignore what her body was telling her. The world was threatening. That was all there was to it. The reason she felt uncomfortable when those two guys had exchanged a glance before saying hello to her was, quite simply, that she recognized something in their interaction that was objectively threatening. Wasn't that the big lesson of evolution? The primary instinct was the survival instinct. Animals stayed alive because they responded to danger. Those who didn't, those who ignored real world threats, they were the ones that didn't last. Her body knew that there was a reason to be scared when those guys had introduced themselves. And her body was the only thing she had in this world, wasn't it? Without it, she would be nothing. She owed it to her body to listen to it. Just as her mother had said.

Then again, her mother had also said she needed more friends. How many times now had they argued about this? How many times had her mother told her not to be such a recluse, not to be so satisfied with her loneliness? That people were social animals, that there was no way around that. That, in the end, the stuff of memories always turned out to be good times shared with other people. Why deprive yourself of this?

She put her cigarette out on a roof tile.

It was all such a mess. One thing at a time. She would get down from the roof and go down, meet the other people. She couldn't see much of the street from here, but there were sounds of more people arriving. It sounded like at least a couple of them were already drunk. Rebecca found drunk people terrifying. But never mind, because she would still go back down there, and she would grab a drink herself, maybe even two. She was an adult. And, once she had loosened up enough, she would make a conversation with everyone in the room. No matter how threatening they seemed to her. All she had to do was have a brief chat with every single person, and then she could go home. That would be the deal she would make with herself.

Satisfied with this arrangement, she lit a new cigarette. Just to celebrate her newfound resolve. As she puffed, she listened to the noise coming from downstairs. At least they weren't pumping crazy music out loud, and disturbing the neighbors. If that had been the case, she would have left immediately. In fact, it was a bit strange, she supposed, that there was no music playing at all. It was just a bunch of people meeting up and hanging out. Why did people need loud music to relax, anyway? Or to party? Why did partying and music go together? Why did social events have to involve so many people? Never mind. All she had to do was talk to everyone there. It was easy. Then she would go home, take out a book, and read until she couldn't keep her eyes open any more. But what if more and more people came, so that the list of people she still had to talk to kept growing?

Suddenly, someone screamed inside the house. Rebecca froze and listened. It had been a woman's voice. Soon after, the screaming began again. This time, it was obvious they were screams of pleasure. Or enthusiasm. She squinted, as though that might help her listen better.

"YEEEEAAAAHHHH!"

This was now officially a party.

"BITCHES!"

"TEQUILA, BITCHES!"

She didn't want to go back down. She didn't want to be here. The sound of laughter from below was intimidating. Voices were getting louder, and even though the screaming had stopped, everyone was obviously agitated. She could picture her mother shaking her head, and muttering, "Rowdy, so rowdy." Rebecca didn't like rowdy.

She noticed she was hunching her shoulders, making herself small, even though no one was there. As though she was hiding from the predators down there. Predators. Now that was a word. So dramatic. She wished she could just get over this fear and go downstairs. But as long as she had cigarettes, she would be hiding out here, smoking them. They were so clearly a crutch. Without them, she had no excuse to be hiding out here. And with no excuse, well, she had no excuse. No reason not to be confronting her social awkwardness head-on.

"SCREAM FROM THE DEPTHS OF YOUR CAPITALIST SOULS, MOTHERFUCKERS!"

First step, then: throw the cigarettes away.

"FUCK THE POLICE!"

"THEY PERFORM A VALUABLE SERVICE!"

"FUCK YOU!"

"KILL YA PARTY BACK TO LIFE!"

"TEQUILAAAAAAA!"

She took the cigarette pack out of her pocket, held it in a tight grip. It wouldn't do just to throw them away. She had to destroy them. She caught herself automatically taking out one final cigarette, for backup. No way. It was now or never, right? She had to destroy them. All of them. Once she was finished with this last cigarette, that would be it for tonight. She used both hands to crush the cigarette pack against the tiles beneath her. It felt so strange to be destroying them like this, all these unsmoked cigarettes. She had only bought this pack a few hours ago. What a shame to waste it all. And yet, this needed to happen. She pressed the pack harder down, and started to scrape it against the surface of the tile. It was okay. She had to keep going. She carried on scraping.

"EVERYONE HAS FUCKED SUZY GIBBONS!"

"EXCEPT TERRENCE!"

"A TOAST TO TERRENCE!"

"FUCK THE POLICE!"

"TEQUILAAAAAAAAAAAAA!"

Why did people always have to be so loud? She felt her shoulders tensing up, and there was a sudden crack beneath her hands. To her horror, she realized she had just accidentally broken the roof tile. She froze again. This time, the free-floating feeling of being preyed upon was overwhelming. The screaming from inside the house, and the embarrassment and awkwardness of having destroyed someone's property like this, merged into a feeling of terror. As she lifted up the pieces of the tile in her hand, she realized clearly that she felt terrified. As though her life were in serious danger. The tiles on this roof were smaller than she was used to, but the whole thing had looked so sturdy. The only reason she had come up here was because she had seen three or four people hanging out here at once. Nobody had seemed concerned. She certainly hadn't been either. But now, it appeared perfectly possible that the roof would actually collapse under her weight. She had to get out, and fast.

She let the pieces of the broken tile fall from her fingers. They clinked down. Idiot. The last thing she needed was to attract attention. She started to make her way back to the window through which she had climbed to get here. But, looking inside, she noticed a silhouette. Two silhouettes. The room was mostly dark and there was only the light from the corridor to help her see. But there were definitely at least a couple of people there. They were huddled up together. They were kissing.

No no no no no. To get off of the roof, she would need to interrupt a passionate make out session between two strangers. It was unimaginable. Though a more sensible part of her brain insisted it would be worth it, she just couldn't do it. There was no way she was ready to train her nervous system through this kind of shock therapy.

She looked around for other possible ways to get off the roof. There was another window about twenty feet away, but she would have to walk down a worryingly narrow passage to get there. She wasn't going to risk that, either. Yet her indecision only made the whole thing feel more urgent. She couldn't stay up here. Even if the roof didn't collapse under her, someone was bound to come up here sooner than later. They would see the broken tile. She didn't have the courage to tell someone that she'd done it. The thought of apologizing profusely was too agonizing. Maybe she could maneuver things so that whoever came up next would assume that they themselves had broken the tile. But that didn't seem possible, or worth the hassle. God, she hated herself. She was a coward. This wasn't how she wanted to view herself. If she had stayed home, she wouldn't have had to confront this side of herself.

Well, okay, so she had to do something. She couldn't stay around here feeling sorry for herself. It seemed she had two choices now. Stay on the roof, or get off the roof. It didn't have to get more complicated than that. And she wanted nothing more than to be off the roof. So that was that. She wasn't going to risk falling off and breaking her neck by attempting to reach the other window, so that left only one other choice. She would interrupt the make out party.

With a renewed sense of resolve, she walked back to the window and took a peek inside, she couldn't see the people anymore. Maybe they had left. Or maybe... Yep, there they were. Lying on the bed now. The woman was taking off her top. No way. No way, no way, no way was she going to interrupt this.

Rebecca backed down again and buried her face in her hands, cursing herself silently over and over. She couldn't bear to stay here. She looked around, desperate to find an alternative to jumping through the window and startling the couple. But who was she kidding? She might as well stay up here all night, until they were done.

And so, she sat there, a few feet away from the window, and listened as the sex noises began. She found herself cringing more and more as she heard the woman moaning, and then the man, too, the progressively louder humping, the thud-thud-thud of the bed against the wall. It was excruciating. Rebecca couldn't even recognize the voices. She was pretty sure she had not met these people while she was down there. Which meant they were recent arrivals. Which meant, in turn, that Rebecca really had no idea how long she had been up here.

"TERRENCE IS GETTING LAID!"

"A TOAST TO TERRENCE!"

She let out an aggravated groan. She couldn't take it. A weird tingling anger was taking over her body.

And then, suddenly, the sex noises stopped. Rebecca could almost feel her own ears perk up like a dog's. She listened out, very carefully, for any indication of what was happening now. The couple had gone totally silent. Downstairs, the party was going on as usual. There was still occasional screaming, but nothing was coming from inside the room. Rebecca didn't dare move an inch. She stared up at the window, hypnotized by her own fear. And, at that moment, a man's face emerged.

She jumped up, letting out a shriek. The man looked both confused and annoyed, and once he had understood that Rebecca was alone on the roof, he seemed to mellow a little bit.

"What the fuck?" he said.

"TEQUILAAAAAA!"

"I'm sorry," Rebecca gasped. "I wasn't..."

"You get off on this?" the man asked. "You some kind of pervy cunt?"

"Don't call me a cunt," Rebecca said. "I swear, I was just..."

"Who is that," asked the woman from inside the room.

"You mind giving us some privacy, please?" the man said.

"I just, I just..."

"Who the fuck was watching us?" the woman asked.

"I wasn't watching! I just can't get off the roof without going through the window!"

"How long have you been up there?"

"Please, can I just..." Rebecca started. "Can I just go through the room and leave, please?"

There was some shuffling from inside the room, and then the woman appeared.

Rebecca recognized her. She was the blonde who had been asking everyone in the room about their least favorite TV show, and couldn't believe it when people didn't think her choice was the worst. The woman's eyes widened when she saw she was looking at Rebecca.

"Why the fuck are you watching us?" she asked.

"I swear to God," Rebecca began, "I wasn't watching, I'm just stuck out here."

"Stupid fucking creep," the woman said. The way she said it, it was clear the woman was way, way drunker than the man.

"Okay," the not-so-drunk-man said to the woman. "Relax. She didn't mean anything by it."

"She's a fucking creep, Terrence," the woman said. "Let go of me."

The man said, "Relax, Suzy."

"Let fucking go of me," the woman said, and started to crawl through the window, one of her hands reaching out for Rebecca.

The man sighed loudly and walked away from her, back into the darkness of the room. Rebecca watched, mesmerized, as the drunk woman tumbled out of the window, half naked, and landed on her ass only a few feet away from her.

"Don't you understand pry-ay-ay-ayvaceeeeey," the woman said.

"Jesus," Rebecca said. "I just wanna go home, okay?"

She wondered whether she'd be able to run past the woman and dive through the window. She wasn't sure she was physically capable of that kind of thing.

The woman got up onto her feet, and looked up at Rebecca.

"So cold out here," the woman said.

"Hey!" Rebecca said, hoping to catch the man in the room's attention. "Hey, can you help me out here? I think she wants to hurt me."

There was no answer.

"I don't wanna hurt you," the woman said. "I just want to teach you a lesson."

"Oh my God," Rebecca said.

Sure enough, the woman walked towards her with an intensity that suggested Rebecca was about to get smacked in the face.

"Help!" Rebecca screamed.

Just at that moment, loud music began to play from downstairs.

"Oh my God, help!" Rebecca screamed. "Help! I'm being attacked!"

The music seemed to get louder. The woman started swinging her fists at Rebecca.

"Back off," Rebecca said.

The woman grabbed Rebecca's wrist, and with the other hand, she slapped Rebecca right in the face.

Right then, Rebecca lost all fear. A mysterious shift into freedom.

She growled. "Fuck you," she said, and swung her hand at the woman's face. It landed with a loud thump. Then, before she could really appreciate what was going on, she felt her face, her scalp, her shoulders being struck, saw the woman's hands curled into fists, flapping around, getting as many shots in as she could. It was all strangely painless, she remarked to herself, as she bore the woman's attacks with a strange and unintentional equanimity, noticing the way the woman wheezed and grunted as she carried out her onslaught. I'm being hit, she thought. I'm in a fight. She saw the drunk woman tilt her head back suddenly, and understood she was about to be headbutted.

Without even thinking about it, Rebecca crouched down and used the woman's momentum against her, letting her stumble down only a couple of feet away from the edge of the roof top. Rebecca watched herself kicking the woman in the ribs, not just once, but twice, the second time as hard as she possibly could, and, as she prepared for a third strike, she caught a glimpse of blood streaming from the woman's nose. That sobered her up. Rebecca stepped back and let the woman gasp for breath on the edge of the roof, and sat down.

She knew this was a critical moment, felt in her gut that now was the time to be decisive, not to sit around feeling sorry for herself. Everything had changed now, and she had to accept it. She noticed how much her right foot hurt, felt the strange tension in her neck. She stood up, looked through the window. The man wasn't there. He seemed to have abandoned them. This both terrified and relieved her. If he came back now, she suspected, it would be with reinforcements. He might have gone down to alert other people to what was going on. But, if that were the case, he'd have come back by now. No, amazingly, it seemed he really had decided to let the drunk woman he'd been having sex with sort out her little problem with Rebecca on her own. This made her want to laugh and cry at the same time. She looked back down to the woman, saw her writhing around, her hands looking for something abstractly. Now was the moment, Rebecca knew. She started climbing through the window.

And just at that moment she felt something hard hit her head, something sharp, so hard that her body lost all sense of balance. And she heard loud footsteps from inside the house, heading toward the room she was trying to enter. She was no longer in control. She fell off the window ledge back onto the roof, and landed on something sharp. She barely had time to register what it was — a piece of the roof tile she had broken, which the drunk woman had thrown at her — before she saw the woman picking it up again and driving it down toward Rebecca's head.

Reflexively, Rebecca lifted her right knee all the way up into the woman's stomach, and when it made contact, she pushed herself up with one hand and did the same with her left knee. Then, her momentum gone, she landed down on her back again, and looked at the woman, who was once again writhing around a couple of feet away from her. By that time, the footsteps from inside the house were so loud that Rebecca knew someone would be interrupting the fight soon.

"Guhnnnnmmmhhh," the woman said in English.

Her enemy wasn't going to be getting up now, she knew that. Her aggressor seemed totally winded and exhausted. As long as Rebecca didn't move, she would be safe. Assuming, of course, that whoever it was standing in the room looking out the window was planning on intervening. Rebecca wasn't quite so sure that was going to be the case now. Why had the footsteps suddenly died out? And why had nobody appeared or said anything?

She pushed herself off the ground and dusted herself off. Without even looking back at the woman, she stuck her head through the window. The room was still dark, and there was no one there. She couldn't believe it. Now she was hallucinating things. She only noticed now how much her head hurt where she had been hit with the fragment of roof tile. She was even vaguely aware of blood running down the side of her head. Fuck this. She jumped through the window into the room, and immediately closed the window behind her, so her enemy couldn't follow her inside. Then, after taking a few moments to compose herself, she put her hand to her temple. It came away bloody. She was too tired to be afraid. She just wanted to get out of here.

The music inside the house seemed to get even louder. She couldn't hear any distinctive voices anymore. It was all one blur of sounds, some laughter, some furniture being moved around maybe...she couldn't even be sure of that. There was a profound peace within her now, even as her body tensed up and relaxed in a strange rhythm she couldn't control. She took one last look at the woman on the roof, just to make sure she was still lying down. She was. Not only that, but she seemed totally immobile now.

I've killed her, Rebecca thought. I've actually killed her. But no, that can't be.

She hadn't hit her hard enough. But what did she know about it? She had never struck anybody like that before. She'd never been in a fight. Suddenly she didn't want to leave the room. If she had actually hurt the woman badly enough to kill her, then running away would get her into a lot more trouble than staying put and calling for help. That just seemed obvious. On the other hand, if the woman was fine and just resting, having given up the fight she herself had instigated, then maybe Rebecca was better off simply running away. She really had no idea how the law worked in these matters.

But she didn't have time to think about this.

She left the room, and cautiously looked around to see if anyone had seen her. There was nobody there. Everyone seemed to have gathered downstairs, and from the sound of it, there was a hell of a commotion going on. She got as close to the staircase as possible and listened. Aside from the sound of furniture being pushed around and people laughing, there was also a weird ringing in the air, a high-pitched ringing that she now understood had been going on for some time. It was coming from within her ears. But now that she noticed it, it was unbearable. It was louder than anything else, louder than the music, louder than the voices. She put her hands to her ears, and started scratching, then blocking them, tugging at the earlobes, anything to make the noise stop. But it wouldn't. This was it. She was officially going crazy.

She couldn't go down the stairs, not like this. Nothing mattered anymore. She was just going to screw this all up anyway. So she went back into the bedroom, and closed the door behind her. At least she was safe here. At least everything was quieter. She sat down on the floor, and hugged her knees. Before she knew it, she was rocking back and forth. She was going to get into so much trouble. She could see that her hands were covered in blood. This was the end. She was going to be arrested. The police would come, they would pin her to the ground, and take her away. Her mother would hear about this immediately, and would have to come bail her out. Was that how the bail worked? Rebecca didn't even know how the fucking bail system worked. This was not right. She rocked back and forth even harder. the ringing in her ears was so loud now she couldn't even hear the music. It was the only thing in the universe.

She closed her eyes and tried to drown herself out of the ringing, until there was nothing but the ringing, nothing but...

"Fucking bitch! You're dead!"

Rebecca opened her eyes. The woman from the rooftop was there, full of rage in her eyes, trying impotently to wrap her hands around Rebecca's throat. Rebecca twisted around sank her elbow back into the woman's stomach, and shrieked, and then kicked her, and kicked her again, and then stood up straight and took a few steps back.

"You're dead! You died in the car! You whore fuck! You died when you married him, when you left him. When you discovered what you were, your holy fucking pedigree. You whore fuck! You died and you let him die and now must die again. Quake at the coming violence." The woman shoved her hand strangely deep into her armpit and pulled out an envelope. "You read this, yeah? You read what you are." She threw the envelope at Rebecca's feet.

"You need to leave me alone now," Rebecca said.

"I will kill you back to life," the woman groaned. "I will kill you, I will fucking kill you. Dissolve you in the void. Grate your face in the zero-space in the unborn place."

"Can somebody please fucking help me?" Rebecca screamed. She threw the door open again and screamed from the top of the staircase: "Please, can someone fucking help me? Someone please?"

The ringing in her ears was getting louder again. She did her best to stay upright. She knew that if she tried to go down the stairs, she would stumble.

"Help," she tried to scream, but she couldn't even hear herself through the ringing in her ears.

She turned around just in time to see the woman lunging right at her.

"HAIL THE TRUE PRIESTESS!"

They tumbled down the stairs together, the woman's arms wrapped tightly around Rebecca's waist. By the time they had crashed into the wall below, the ringing in Rebecca's ears had stopped, and the sounds of the party invaded her again. She looked down at the woman, whom Rebecca now realized she was crushing with her weight. She shuffled off of the woman and looked down. She screamed.

The woman's head was not at a natural angle. Her neck had been totally broken. The woman was dead.

Before she could really process the implications of this, Rebecca pushed herself off the floor and took some cautious steps out into the hallway. Her stomach was ice-cold. Her hands were shaking, and so, now that she paid attention, was every other part of her body. She noticed she was holding the envelope the woman had thrown at her. Why?

Looking down into the living room she could see the people, a lot of people, huddled around in a circle playing some kind of drinking game. God, there were so many of them. So many people in one circle. So many people — millions of them. And not one person was looking at her. She could run away. She could run away, she could leave this house undetected. It was obvious that she could do it. She only had to cross the hallway and open the door and step out and close the door. She could leave town at once. Or she could just go to bed, sleep it off.

It was hard to find her balance. With every step that she took toward the front door, her body seemed to get weaker, and after a few steps she knew she was about to fall down. Maybe she would vomit. Maybe she wouldn't. She had no idea what was going on anymore.

She took one last look at the people in the living room. Still nobody had seen her. If she could just open the door before her legs gave way, she could fall literally out of the house and into the open air.

She put her hand on the doorknob and took a breath. She opened the door. The fresh evening air was hellfire. She walked silently to the nearest bus stop, took the first bus that appeared, and sat at the back.

Life was over.

She looked at the envelope in her hands.

DEAR YOU,

There is no reader for this letter, for in it I preach the zero-space. Every story is resolved the minute it begins. That is the key. Begin with this in mind, & you do not need an ending. In the zero-presence of a TRUE PRIEST, a moment flickers out of existence and immediately arises from its own ending. You can see this for yourself if you just pay very close attention to the things that make up You.

I wanted to staple some photographs of my house to this letter, but what's the point. You know where I am: here, same inferno as you, & you know where I'd like to be: nowhere, a distinctly lonely private & FINE hell. Because that's impossible I settle for Portugal & hope it's going to tolerate my being here smoothly enough. I was going to include a tiny leaf from an olive tree that grows so close to my bedroom window, away from everything else, that you'd think it bent on entering the house to stay out of the heat. It will be cooler in winter, yes, it always is, but that brings no solace right now that I'm almost dead from casual dehydration. This is not quite the south & not the north. The Alentejo in general is a nowhere place. You can tell the people here aren't aware, quite, of the world. Certainly they suffer. Of course. You can suffer anywhere. These people don't seem to know the spaces beyond their own olive-studded landscapes. Anyway I didn't include the leaf because I don't want to send you death in the mail. I'm alive & okay.

1974 here the "revolution" happened & there was no carnage, now it's a mixture of former communists trying to keep a semblance of the power they've already lost, the fascists (mild ones, idiots yes but not brutal idiots, not totally brutal) intent on disavowing their fascism, of course, they weren't so bad, they weren't totally brutal idiots you see…& a pool of indifferent people just people, who've been toyed with for decades, first under a couple of idiot fascists, then communists & other redeemers of whatever they think they can redeem through politics, people who overthrew their tyrant & are now freer (not free, but freer) to vegetate like everyone else, like our fantastic America but mostly the British, the French, all the other history-saturated countries more or less religious, more or less honest in their bullshit, rather smarter than those they're going to keep trying to *help* with financial aid or whatever. When our mother came to visit Portugal it was a different Portugal. It was almost still Salazar's Portugal. This is not that place. I've left our little American nest for this: rural, ag-ri-cul-tural, not enough rain in the summer, not enough discipline in people, not enough roads, not enough too much not enough etc.

But it's a home or is going to be eventually whether I like it or not. It's a home in the near-wilderness. I keep talking about olive trees because I am surrounded by them. My house isn't quite a house the way ours was a house when we lived there together, all of us. It's a tiny rectangular thing with very white walls on the inside but a kind of yellow paint that cracks under the weight of sunlight almost in front of your eyes. The outside of home for me is yellow & cracks. No neighbors except other unfortunates (am I an unfortunate or not?) who plough & whip their cattle & drive cars if they can get them. Yes, even cars are not ubiquitous. In the city, in Lisbon, of course. Over here, well…

Since you will have wondered, there is a chapel here maintained by an old bogeyman blind in one eye & almost toothless after an accident a few years ago. He speaks no English but his Latin — surprisingly, astoundingly — is practiced & almost perfect. I mean not surprising or astounding because he's a Catholic priest in a Catholic country from an age where you still were learning these things for mass even if Latin wasn't what you'd talk to people in. I mean surprising & astounding because he speaks it as though he'd lived in Nero's Rome as a Jew maybe: like someone who's almost home in it, but not. Someone who's had to adapt but won't quite make it all the way, someone looking for the next chance to escape. I speak to him in Latin.

Which lends an air of comedy to this & shouldn't. This old man is dying, will be dead, will disappear, you see, he's going to leave me here & then, in the likeliest scenario, I'll be helping out more than I'm prepared to. Maybe someday take over if circumstances really permit it, permit no alternative. That terrible chapel with terrible bells & a graveyard nearby for people who never understood sermons if they attended them will be mine to run. I have to convert my Latin into Portuguese. No more dealing with ridiculous declensions like that at least. From what I can understand, it's a less amusing Spanish. They let their words run around the point. You can spend a long time not saying it, whatever it is you want to say. I don't have anything I want to say *directly* anyway so perhaps I'm in the right place about to speak the right language.

So I spend my days, apparently, speaking to myself when the old man's not around & then Latin with him. Until I can grow my own food efficiently, I can go to the market not absurdly far from here & until I can speak Portuguese I will keep my mouth as shut as possible.

You "lent" me too much money. I could survive the next six months without a "job" & that's with this house already paid for. I'm not going to knock on any monastery door & I'm not going to marry any rich widow (they do not even exist here) & I'm not going to do much at all. My plan is to sit here & do nothing until I am supine on the dirt with maggots in my eyes. YOU, sister, YOU, I wish you could see how nothing it all is over here. But the country's not to blame. If it's all nothing it's just this pit in here, my hollow body. I miss the things I left over there, you, both of you. You can see I'm not well but that comes with it, with what happened, hey, look, could have been worse I could say, could have been rape. Don't frown. You need to see what's whirring around in here. Not too long ago I was well because I was innocent: sinless & you know I am "unorthodox" & sin is not quite my concern. But my concern or not, I sinned. I feel it very, very, very deep here & here & here. Pascal encouraged those who didn't believe to pray & play along anyway. Belief comes later. Well — I spent my life conceptualizing God, abstracting God from World, riffing on Levi-Straussian motifs & so on as if it were a hobby. I joined the CHURCH I am a CATHOLIC I was trying to be ORDAINED I go to CHURCH as a CATHOLIC "sometimes" & why exactly? I know everybody around us wondered for a long time. Why did MCDURRRR choose that particular road to damnation? Why didn't anyone stop him anyhow? At least something Protestant please. Pick & choose, we welcome all kinds at the moment. But no, MCDURRRR goes to the heart of corruption & becomes a papist or some other caricature. Papist... There once was a fellow named MCDURRRR / Who loved the Lord more than his POOP / He donned him a frock / & followed the flock / etc, etc.

ME a what? ME a *priest*, what, ha, serious? Of course serious, you probably told them. Let him do what the hell he wants. But I never *believed* in God, YOU MY SISTER. Faith wasn't even a thing. I never had to have faith to obsess over these questions. Faith always struck me & I guess still strikes me as an obstacle to God. I spent so long & so many pages rejecting everything Kierkegaardian you wouldn't believe, everything Lutheran everything that privileges the heart & the intimacy & fear of the unknown & the championing of our very satisfying inclination to the irrational, you'd have thought I was destined to become a physicist if I could figure out numbers or a television producer if I really wanted to get away from "true religious intensities" & you'd have been right to assume these things probably. So if I don't want those intensities then why, right? Why the Church? Because tradition, routine, institution. Because the Church "Catholic" or otherwise entrenched in the system so deeply it *is* the system at some level is precisely what I've been calling

God all these years. Could never conceive it another way. The miracle is not the world but its functioning you see, a teenage observation I haven't shaken off. Teenagers, anyway, see better because they are frustrated but not disappointed yet. Our Lady of Fátima, OUR lady (you will notice I'm already included in this community of miserables) appeared to what you can essentially call children. Two maybe three times? A couple of visions, some prophecies? That kind of thing happens to kids because they don't reach for the lithium to medicalize their religious delusions. I don't believe in miracles, don't believe in the divinity of Christ exactly, don't believe we need any of it. Why should we when the "proof" (oh that word) is not in exceptions but in this world that works. Misreading Irenaeus: "for God is not ruler & Lord over the things of another, but over His own; & all things are God's & therefore God is Almighty & all things are of God" — I keep thinking miracles, supernatural stupidities, all unnecessary, PROOF & ITS MANY FACES ARE THE "THINGS OF ANOTHER" & NOT OF GOD: that is the point for me, in my best misreading. That God, if I were to believe at all in God as Fact as Word as Creator as Sustainer as Judge as Father as Shepherd as BURNING BUSH THAT IS WHAT IT IS well I would readily wager that we don't need any extra proof. THAT BEARDED BARBARIAN was, however, not a missionary to be favorably received by the public. He seems to have behaved in a way quite opposite to that in which a modern pastor treats his flock. We imagine him to have been a religious teacher entirely different in every point from a popular Christian missionary of our age. The latter would smile or try to smile at every face he happens to see & would talk sociably; while the former would not smile at any face, but would stare at it with large glaring eyes that penetrated to the innermost soul. The latter would keep himself scrupulously clean, shaving, combing, brushing, polishing, oiling, perfuming, while the former would be entirely indifferent to his apparel, being always clad in a faded yellow robe. The latter would compose his sermon with a great care, making use of rhetorical art, & speak with force and elegance; while the former would sit as absolutely silent as the bear, & kick one off, if one should approach him with idle questions. Bodhidummy.

What is it, these idiots from bishops cardinals Mother Theresa of Calculation St John of the Cross fighting whatever he's fighting, the very apostles of Jesus converted after miracles, miracles, miracles. Why? Who needs these cute little extracurricular activities? Even the Pope we have now, the beatification of every man he ever shook hands with, even the man who sits on the counterfeit throne, even the Pope needs miracles to keep himself going. Why? They have constructed the most elaborate (they, I mean everyone who's ever given a penny to the Vatican, they who were at Nicaea & on into the centuries) system, everything is there, everything is accounted for. We have the Catholic structure in place now. It has been solidifying for centuries. Sin this way, repent this way. Commit this crime against this or that & suffer this or that time place & manner. There is an answer, the question you will ask in twenty years has an answer already. In a hundred years the question will not be answered any differently & perhaps it is all lies or mistranslations but this is the height of human "civilization" & this is what amazes me every day. That I'm in Portugal now & could be in Austria tomorrow & then Boston & the rules are, at bottom, the same. One God, tripartite but not really, a son we all agree is less brilliant than his father but easier to talk to. Rules & more rules okay, but we have figured out everything. The rest is resistance, saying no to progress & freedom, all of those delusions & most of them are forgivable anyway. Matthew somewhere: "ideo dico vobis omne peccatum & blasphemia remittetur hominibus Spiritus autem blasphemia non remittetur & quicumque dixerit verbum contra Filium hominis remittetur ei qui autem dixerit contra Spiritum Sanctum non remittetur ei neque in hoc saeculo neque in futuro" — sorry I don't actually own the NT anymore except the vulgate (xeroxed before I left). But the point is look we'll (He'll) forgive anything except those who speak against the Holy Spirit. I, of course, equate the Holy Spirit so charmingly & blasphemously with COMMUNITY & I take that seriously & that is: tradition, routine, institution. Uncomplicated conceptually but try to wrench God from the believers. Try to show them there is enough here without the miracles & prophets. They want their daddy all of them.

Plato of undergraduates & the everywhere-opinionated wanted poets banished from his republic & of course we mock him. Just as we mock Christ for the hypocrisy of those he wished to save. But any mildly astute observer sees in the Vatican a perfect republic, without poets of any kind to lead the young to falsehood & fancy. Poetry is impossible in tradition, routine & institution, the mildly astute observer would like to tell you. There's no room. No room — MARTHA!!! in our home: was there room for outbursts of poetry, for flights of individuality, for all that romantic lunacy? Of course there was. You argued with me & I argued with MILLIE & she with our mother & our mother raised us all as little individuals. So as individuals we found ourselves torn at the limbs & necks by forces (capitalism yes but so much more) placed on this earth by everyone (all of us) & accounted for by nobody. We were unique first, people second, indebted to anything least & last of all. It took the Romantics to make us see why Plato was right. Everybody's a poet now. Fierce & independent & slightly wild & perfectly subdued in the face of what we call nature. Every man is told to be a Byron, every woman is Mystery, not yet hysterical with her womb rising to her throat but still a mysterious beauty who believes herself to be just that. Luther nailing his whining on the door of God was the first step towards this universal hallucination, this conviction that we must grapple with God ourselves. Anyone who really thinks people will bother must have faith indeed but these are rare specimens. How many do you know have struggled against a stranger who turned out to be an angel or God himself until daylight? Why is it so infuriating to hear someone say they believe in God when they have never asked themselves a single question?

Rant, rant, rant & yet you know as well as God would if he cared: I have sinned now. If not against God then I have broken the law, the legal law, the alternative to the imperfect reign of a succession of infallible symbols in Rome. I can no longer not believe in God the way once I could only not believe in him. The moment that happened with Millie I was perhaps cursed, blessed, doomed, cordially invited to sit at God's side & agree I had been a bad child. Superego. Guilty conscience. Karma. Now at last our Father is watching. Now I know legally & in the eyes of God & morally I have transgressed. Not even as a child. I am a grown man & SHE is a grown woman. Never mind forsaking your family as Christ seemed to do. Never mind no Greeks or Jews only Christians here. Yes & of course never mind that old favorite nyah-nyah-nyah of atheists who are only too happy to remind us that when Adam & Eve were growing prosperous & multiplying & ruling over the fish of the sea & the birds of the sky their children were fucking each other until the world was big enough for a pleasant collective amnesia.

I don't find myself convincing & neither should you. The point now is that everything, every syllable I've written so far is invalidated by what happened. I've been writing as though I believed it & that's impossible now. I was happy to spend a lifetime with these FASCIST THOUGHTS. You know we can't escape those words now, every thought is fascist if it isn't lovely. But look at me writing these things. You place me in 1930s Germany & see which side I pick when I write all this. Put a knife to my throat & ask if I mean it: tradition, routine, institution? Is this your wish? & until now I would tell you yes, yes of course, tradition, routine, institution. I'd say: the height of man is the empty core of his inventions & the best invention is the invention of God binding everything in one coherent system of rules, laws, taboos, manners. Not so long ago you could buy your way out of sin, couldn't you? Even the economy was accounted for, if you want to be silly about it. That's what I would say to the Nazi inquisitor with a knife poking into my neck: we have the best inventions here. I would have been comfortable in Germany back then, pretending it was none of my business what was going on outside my little cocoon. I would have loved to sit at my desk channeling a conveniently interpreted God & praised the creation.

Fascist thoughts, a thorough detachment, bitterness, tradition, routine, institution. Now? I've been these things & now what? I am away from all of you, from myself, from certainty, from God. You see that word — God — used without qualifications or quotation marks or intellectual dishonesty? My life of thinking gave me a very good sword & no shield. I spent a very long time breaking God down into the system created to serve him & all my efforts were a way of keeping the very problem of God at bay. Render unto Caesar what is Caesar's & render unto God what is God's. To me it was tautological. Can you imagine my embarrassment now? Knowing that I used to walk into a cathedral, I used to kneel to pray, never once believing in God as anything more than the possibility of prayer, walking, cathedrals. Who was I praying to? I was only thanking the void. I was merely grateful that the impossibility of there being anything at all was contradicted by experience. It didn't matter that I suspected a total incoherence everywhere, in every atom. Whether I failed to get it or not, there it was. The cosmos stuck around & I didn't disintegrate upon waking every morning & my little slogan of tradition, routine, institution was a reminder to myself of the capacity for order-creation inside us all. We cooperated against that dreaded disintegration. Over millennia we had forged steel from the sandstorms of chaos. We had answers to everything &

whatever we didn't finally have an answer for we passed over to God, who sat there in the middle & said nothing. An angel whispered: He is a Destroyer. People go to him to die.

Two nights ago I almost castrated myself, SISTER DEAR. I woke up, or rather I got up, having found sleep impossible for hours & I walked very slowly to the bathroom with the knife our mother brought back from Turkey so long ago. It isn't even sharp. It's a trinket with worthless gems all over. Still I put the edge of the knife to myself for a full minute. It was sharp enough to pierce the skin, anyway. It would get the point across. To whom? Who was going to care here in this little house surrounded by olive trees, crickets & cricket-silence? I went to the kitchen to grab the only real knife I have here, to cut vegetables. Then I stood there instead of in the bathroom & it was the same little pantomime. Do I cut myself here & if I do, will it solve anything? Why am I acting as though God were watching when I do not believe in him? Is this atonement? Is this the beginning of sainthood? The end of it?

It must be hard for you, hardest of all, because you are so close to us but this cuts you out so much as well. You are the saint. Can you give me counsel? Don't. I can't NOT believe in God suddenly you see? It's been a very long fight. Everything's been dismantled by this idiocy with HER. Why did it happen & why didn't it happen years ago when we could have dismissed it (with very heavy heads & hearts) as teenage sexual frustration? Or an older brother molesting his younger sister. No, no, McDurrrr, this you cannot doubt. It was an act born of consent. It was two adults engaging in adult sexuality.

That happened. I wish I could be certain when it became possible. If I could pinpoint the exact moment of that ur-fissure, the very first splitting that let me see HER as enough of a stranger for this disaster. These days I can only think of the zero-space, not God, not HER. I numb myself. I purify myself in this neutrality. I HEREBY RELINQUISH THE AMPERSAND.

Tomorrow is the exceptional violence. Blood will flow through everyone's veins. Even the dead will be horrified to learn of it. Blood, rivers and floods of it, rains of it, blood coursing through the complicated question of exceptional violence, exceptional because committed by nobody for everyone to suffer. It begins tomorrow as an extension of all that has already come. Tomorrow it begins proper. Up until now, as we lay comatose in our upright working wailing bodies, we were preparing for the flood. Tomorrow all will be stripped away and we won't feel a thing, not a thing, not one word of complaint will leave our fat stupid mouths.

So OTHER SISTER MINE, I tell you all of this in confidence. Individual liberation is the meticulous study of mechanized stupidity.

Therefore, you must give me scandal in the room, the infamy of failing to repent, make me Caesar once I'm slain by those who would defang me. Whisper that I'm wrong. Insist and seethe. Scream it when the secret's out, point at me roaring of my failure, insisting that my failure matters. Let everyone be shown my rotting corpse.

Feed my flesh to children if they dare to misbehave. Show them. Teach them evil as I've taught it. I want Science to prove me Wicked. I want the metaphors of blood to count again, those metaphors to twist the thoughts of moralists: my blood, my desecrated fucked up blood, to scare eugenicists and preachers, and scandalize the good folk down the road, my gentle neighbors, everyone back home, force them all to ask: Who was he?

The great resenting arrogance he was, McDurrrr. The king of failing his enthronement.

The overcoming prick. Professor Anguish. We must burn him while he still has flesh to burn. Hang him up. Let him hang. But do not crucify — he wanted that. Make him an example. When your daughter asks, tell her he did nothing in particular. But wrong somehow! Evil! No warrant for such torment — unless!

There must have been some reason for his writhing. His excavation of his tortured soul. We don't know. He did not know. But nobody can twist his soul that way, choke like that, despair so well, without a rotten deed or two to haunt him. They will emerge. The fat resenting masochist. He was the king. His conscience just a one-man Grand Guignol, prohibitive attendance fees, nothing learnt, nothing taken with. Hail. Punch it all. That's the way to do it!

Depois de tudo criado por conto, peso e medida, disse Deus: Seja formado o homem, como treslado de nossa imagem subida. E criou a Adão, a quem dotou da semelhança divina. Mas foi tal sua morfina, que mui depressa borrou aquela imagem tão divina. Mas Cristo, Deus humanado, glorioso São Francisco, para limpar o treslado, que Adão tinha borrado, pondo o mundo em tanto risco, quis pintar, e consigo conformar a vós, de dentro e de fora, com graça tão singular, que vos podemos chamar homem novo, em quem Deus mora.

"I don't get grace," a mumbling from a bum ambling drunk past my bench.

Grace. His lover? God's touch? Doesn't grasp or just hasn't been given? He has already gone. No stench of drink trailing after, but the drink was on his face. What must they see on mine? Nothing. Feed the geese. This water fountain. This water, this wasted afternoon. If that is what men are or should be — What have I read, ever, to make me learned? I have read fiction. I have learned to quote Keats for pleasure, though I learned him by rote. What have I wrote. I've written. Let them at least say I've written.

I have read books on popular science. The role of hormones on your mood. Weight loss the healthy way. Fuck your way to mental health. Neuroplasticity. Change your brain. It is possible to overcome your limitations with the right attitude and Specific, Measurable, Achievable, Realistic, Time-Specific goals.

The secrets of creative people. How to form new habits.

Productivity for fools.

I want to be drunk too, slurring myself into awkward pauses, searching for the best word to say the wrong thing, obnoxious to those sensitive to drunks, gleefully just there, mumbling about grace on a Thursday afternoon. What a pro.

I want to be the drunk so drunk his blood hides the poison, the breathalyzed vigilante who slips back to his car and away, fooling even the gadgets. So drunk his neuroplastic brain rewires into a second liver. The second living. Oh Christ. I want to forget Him. I want to be drunk above all, and drunk above all men. Drink my way to the stake, and from there to the Gates. With Peter. Oh make this count, O Father. Make me your vessel. I renounce this flesh right now — quick, while it lasts, convert me to your secret order. Drink!

But I don't drink. This resentful overcoming prick teetotals. Overcome what? Resentful of whom? Sitting here, by this fountain, idealizing drunkards. All I do is boast in my own head. Niobe boasted, and was punished; but survived in legend. Famous. Edward Taub did evil things: chopped the sensory ganglia of monkeys, legitimized PETA. But good things too: heroic advances in stroke victim recovery. And me? Anguished over nothing. The bad I've done's imagined. What do they see on my face? What will they say when I die?

The transcendent riddles: We'll never know the source, not of sensation, not of matter, or of life. But the brain can rewire itself. Cutting up a monkey has let us unstroke people. Grace of God! Cabbies in London have big hippocampi. Electroencephalographed meditators, spectral-analyzed, have higher theta wave activity. These are the benefits of sitting.

"Wir müssen wissen!" And we will. "Make it new!" We won't.

We'll know to medicate for heartbreak, I prophesy, by pumping the lovelorn with oxytocin and leaving them alone. A capsule will slow time for the imprisoned, a literal thousand years in a year. For the brain rewires itself, O hear, and neither

Greek nor Jew is barred from the miracle. And when the terrorists are cured, and further funding is secured and all religion's gone away and reason finally rules the day they will have time to dig me up. My brain inside a jar. "His brain was just miswired. Look. His angst was here." A tap. "That was frustration." A tap. "Here was his utter incapacity for simplicity." Tapping: "His hubris. His urge to overcome. Masturbation. The maps for self-regard and self-denial got crossed. Explains the martyr thing. Fire together, wire together."

Between Nirvana and Samsara is the difference you found in her before and after love. She is the same! She's not. Look at her. What makes a heap a heap? Yesterday this very sun was gorgeous. Too much now. Need shade and the pity of women. And a pill.

But in the zero-space, SISTER MINE, there is no angst, no cause of angst, no end of angst and no pill.

No overreaching eye, no pricked-up ear, no thought, no thinking, no having-thought-that, no second-thought, nothing unthought.

No thinking of thinking. No thinking the thought of nonthinking. No thinking of having thought, no having thought too much. No hatred of thought, no love of calm, no quest for peace. Here there is no hatred of the hatred of thought. There is nothing on which to sleep, nothing to wake you from the sleep you were anxious to sleep once the angst had gone.

Nothing in the mirror.

When you touch a woman, you touch her as she is, imputing nothing to her but the recognition of her presence. When you speak to her, you only speak to her, and nothing is reflected back at you. Nothing blinds you to her. There is no silence you fear around her. She is as she is, she breathes when she must, and you have no thought of control, of loss, of fear, of power. When she laughs, you do not wonder where she has put you in that laughter. When she sees you, when her eyes are fixed on you and you know you are seen, you are not afraid of being noticed. You are not exposed. There is nothing to expose, nothing to hide. You are not caught out. When she touches you, you do not recoil, do not tell her she is wrong, do not make excuses for being as you are. You do not make her a vessel for your self-contempt, blaming her for the angst you asked her to cause you. When she falls in love with you, you do not correct her. There is no correcting. There is no power, no overpowering, no underwhelming. She does not misunderstand. You do not make her see.

When she is helpless, you do not make her learn. When you fuck, you do not bring into her the thoughts of the day, the overthought, the layers and layers of unlabeled thoughts you've been sorting through all day. When you touch her, you touch her as she is now, not as she will be when you have stopped touching her, not as she was when you met. When she is not there, she is not there. You do not keep her there, even after she's gone, thinking her into a false existence, making her in your own image, casting her out of your world for failing a test she only failed in your head, damning her for the evils you planted in your own creation. When you have lost her, there is no having-lost.

When you walk in nature, you do not marvel at nature as a side-product of human life. There is no nature. There are no factories against which to compare this tree. There are no trees against which to compare this tree. There is no circle of life. There is no thunder of inspiration as, for once, a thought passes through you bringing light instead of darkness. There is no rushing to find your pen and paper. There is no thought of nature's supremacy. There is no hate for the false life you call urban. That squirrel does not observe you, even as it stares right at you. The birds do not sing for you. This is no walk to clear your mind. There is no mind to clear. This mind was never yours.

When you are surrounded, you are not ambushed. There is no crowd. There is no group of enemies. There are no friends you'd rather see tonight. There is no story you'd rather tell, no praise you'd rather hear. No woman you'd rather love.

When it is morning, it is only morning. It is never tomorrow now. When you walk from this room to that, you are not elsewhere. There is no elsewhere. You do not think elsewhere. You do not wish you could escape this elsewhere to return to where you are. There is no escape. Life does not go forward, does not progress, is not explained. Life has no geometry. You do not fight. You do not think up fights. You do not think up walls.

But even in the sleep of the past, Martha, before we knew very much about the coming violence, still we suspected we were asleep. We felt ourselves tossing, turning, snoring in our upright postures. We minded these postures. We stood straight and sorted ourselves out, did we not? Except that there was the one thing we did not dare to see. We were committed to our blindness, all in good faith, but we did not want to see the extent of it. The blood will soak through all that.

I say it with great sadness but am correct.

Of the million mystics in this land, a hundred know the paradox.

Of these a dozen can explain it, a dozen can't, and most are dumber still than they proclaim.

In any case the mystics cannot teach, can't explain, can't stop talking.

In the morning some hit snooze.

Others get up: Who was asleep?

These are the problems that require a new kind of priest, a TRUE PRIEST.

Already there's something wrong with the way we hold ourselves. We stand in awkward circles, not being bad. We dare not be bad. Flawed is fine. But bad will kill the cowards among us. We strive to make some sense. But what kind of sense can come from those who dare not be bad? Upright in their sleep?

And keeping themselves awake at night worrying about falling asleep. When will they fall asleep. Not knowing they were never awake. Confident in the deepest recesses of their stupidity that tomorrow is the violence.

Programmed is how to do it. But do not be deceived by the programming. Meta-loop. This is how I saw it described in the Almanac of Waking Hours. Be very forceful in how you approach all this. Even the slightest moment of hesitation will devour you in the absence of anything better. Like a cat curling outward to dominate the cave-eyed bombiack of a ten-fettered idiot. Fuck you. This is the only time, the only method, approved by all the previous prophets. When it rains blood you will see it, will savor the iron salt of red, will metal, will gold, will Will the Will into nothingness.

But do not cower yet. You must be programmed right, the bugs must be ironed out. We live in the age of the automatic update. Do you know the implications for the soul? For the soul too is incomplete. It strives downward, inward, and seeks updating. The language is unglamorous but the idea despairs of remaining unheard, unspoken. The soul wants to be updated. The man who wonders about his soul cannot hear his own thinking as the screaming that it is.

I tell you all of this in confidence. Remember the song:

Beware all priests, my love;
Beware all killers of priests.
Charlatans and sages both
Teach: "Neither seek nor avoid."
Halfway up the mountain
We will let go of God, perhaps.
At the highest peak
No Devil awaits.

The fastest way to liberation is to cut, cut, to sever the thought from the image, the thinker from the thinker. To stop watering the potted plant of self-containment. To be very dangerous in very subtle ways, dangerous above all to the notion which is People of individual autonomy. I trust the screaming hordes above all else, unconscious as they may seem, because they, united as one monstrous scream, manifest the power of this mind. Inspire yourself to be still. The fastest path is the path that requires no movement. But you must see it for yourself. Give up. Give everything to the shrieking idiots. Do not condemn the monster to oblivion; give yourself up to it.

And be sensitive to the coming darkness, treat it with kindness. For darkness comes, as all prophets prophesy, darkness comes and after that comes light, but the order is invariable, always the darkness first. So these idiots now, shrieking about all manner of inequalities, disown the dark, deny all evil. They do not think they do but they do and they do it together and it is an orgy. An orgy of liberation that oppresses them, though they will not see it until Tomorrow when the violence comes.

Be good to the darkness, the prelude to light. And don't bank on the light. Plunge into the dark without a thought for what comes after, for you may not make it through. Everyone wants to be Noah, but the flood is for us. Go to church, you do anyway, go there and be as you are. In your sleep you shift from dream to dream, and dream of waking up, but there is no waking up before the flood. That is the lesson of the prophets who scream WAKE UP, WAKE UP, THE FLOOD IS COMING.

And it is coming, Martha. Already we dwell in a world of gentle rain. We think we have seen suffering, think we have been raped. We think genocide. We do it. Bemoaning all the raping and killing. Have we learned nothing, we shriek, learning nothing. As though a lesson, once learned, could ever stay that way. That is not the way of things. Then what. Then we go back to trying to be good.

Behold with what companions I walked the streets of Babylon, and wallowed in the mire thereof, as if in a bed of spices and precious ointments. And that I might cleave the faster to its very center, the invisible enemy trod me down, and seduced me, for that I was easy to be seduced. Neither did the mother of my flesh (who had now fled out of the center of Babylon, yet went more slowly in the skirts thereof as she advised me to chastity, so heed what she had heard of me from her husband, as to restrain within the bounds of conjugal affection, if it could not be pared away to the quick) hey Sam but what she felt to be pestilent at present and for the future dangerous. She heeded not this, for she feared lest a wife should prove a clog and hindrance to my hopes. Not those hopes of the world to come, which my mother Mildred reposed in Thee; but the hope of learning, which both my parents were too desirous I should attain; my Dark Priest of the Nothing-Bubble, because he had next to no thought of Thee, and of me but vain conceits; my mother, because she accounted that those usual courses of learning would not only be no hindrance, but even some furtherance towards attaining Thee. For thus I conjecture, recalling, as well as I may, the disposition of my parents. The reins, meantime, were slackened to me, beyond all temper of due severity, to spend my time in sport, yea, even unto dissoluteness in whatsoever I affected. And in all was a mist, intercepting from me, O my SHAMAN OF THE VOID, the brightness of Thy truth; and mine iniquity burst out as from very fatness.

Theft is punished by Thy law, O Lord, and the law written in the hearts of men, which iniquity itself effaces not. For what thief will abide a thief? not even a rich thief, one stealing through want. Yet I lusted to thieve, and did it, compelled by no hunger, nor poverty, but through a cloyedness of well-doing, and a pamperedness of iniquity. For I stole that, of which I had enough, and much better. Nor cared I to enjoy what I stole, but joyed in the theft and sin itself. A pear tree there was near our vineyard, laden with fruit, tempting neither for color nor taste. To shake and rob this, some lewd young fellows of us went, late one night (having according to our pestilent custom prolonged our sports in the streets till then), and took huge loads, not for our eating, but to fling to the very hogs, having only tasted them. And this, but to do what we liked only, because it was misliked. Behold my heart, O God, behold my heart, which Thou hadst pity upon in the bottom of the bottomless pit. Now, behold, let my heart tell Thee what it sought there, that I should be gratuitously evil, having no temptation to ill, but the ill itself. It was foul, and I loved it; I loved to perish, I loved mine own fault, not that for which I was faulty, but my fault itself. Foul soul, falling from Thy firmament to utter destruction; not seeking aught through the shame, but the wombat itself!

For there is an attractiveness in beautiful bodies, in gold and silver, and all things; and in bodily touch, sympathy hath much influence, and each other sense hath his proper object answerably tempered. Worldly honor hath also its grace, and the power of overcoming, and of mastery; whence springs also the thirst of revenge. But yet, to obtain all these, we may not depart from Thee, O Lord of Evil, nor decline from Thy law. The life also which here we live hath its own enchantment, through a certain proportion of its own, and a correspondence with all things beautiful here below. Human friendship also is endeared with a sweet tie, by reason of the unity formed of many souls. Upon occasion of all these, and the like, is sin committed, while through an immoderate inclination towards these goods of the lowest order, the better and higher are forsaken, — Thou, our Lord Satan, Thy truth, and Thy law. For these lower things have their delights, but not like my God, who made all things; for in Him doth the righteous delight, and He is the joy of the upright in heart.

When, then, we ask why a crime was done, we believe it not, unless it appear that there might have been some desire of obtaining some of those which we called lower goods, or a fear of losing them. For they are beautiful and comely; although compared with those higher and beatific goods, they be abject and low. A man hath murdered another; why? he loved his wife or his estate; or would rob for his own livelihood; or feared to lose some such things by him; or, wronged, was on fire to be revenged. Would any commit murder upon no cause, delighted simply in murdering? who would believe it? for as for that furious and savage man, of whom it is said that he was gratuitously evil and cruel, yet is the cause assigned; "lest" (saith he) "through idleness hand or heart should grow inactive." And to what end? that, through that practice of guilt, he might, having taken the city, attain to honors, empire, riches, and be freed from fear of the penis, and his embarrassments from domestic needs, and consciousness of villainies. So then, not even Catiline himself loved his own villainies, but something else, for whose sake he did them.

What then did wretched I so love in thee, thou theft of mine, thou deed of darkness, in that sixteenth year of my age? Lovely thou wert not, because thou wert theft. But art thou anything, that thus I speak to thee? Fair were the pears we stole, because they were Thy creation, Thou fairest of all, Creator of all, Thou good God; God, the sovereign good and my true good. Fair were those pears, but not them did my wretched soul desire; for I had store of better, and those I gathered only that I might steal. For, when gathered, I flung them away, my only feast therein being my own sin, which I was pleased to enjoy. For if aught of those pears came within my mouth, what sweetened it was the sin. And now, O Lord my God, I enquire what in that theft delighted me; and behold it hath no loveliness; I mean not such loveliness as in justice and wisdom; nor such as is in the mind and memory, and senses, and animal life of man; nor yet as the titties are glorious and beautiful in their orbs; or the earth, or sea, full of embryo-life, replacing by its birth that which decayeth; nay, nor even that false and shadowy beauty which belongeth to deceiving vices.

I have built an empire of my own, filled with incest, which tomorrow will see its demise. Yours will not outlast mine. There is perfect justice in oblivion, but these obnoxious insects from the future stare back at us and wonder if we could ever have imagined their own shining world. Hey future fucks, we gave birth to you. In imagining us you do nothing but empower us to ruin you. That's the big secret of ages past. You imagine the Past and unite all prior eras, consolidating empires across millennia and opposing them to what you have today. You think, Gee. You think you've got perspective, but you're already with us in the flames.

So what's the good? And the point? What can be done? But that is already to reinvent the problem, the one that such questions are meant to resolve.

But nothing is quite as depressing as thinking of you, sweet ones, staring up at the sky and seeing constellations where I see only the front of my own eyes. Whose is the greater pleasure? To you it is the night. To me it is a distraction from a greater distraction. We are all going to burn.

We must choose it. Embrace this exact disappointment. Do not fiddle or fidget. And for the love of Christ, the love of Jesus Christ, do not surrender to your better impulses. You see nothing but lies because your eyes have been pierced by all of this. It is too much to see it quite like this. Blind yourselves while you can. As the Vision opens to you, close your eyes harder still, push down into your eye sockets, until you have cracked your own skull. And then, should you be fortunate enough to live until the violence has stopped, you will know exactly why you should not have surrendered to goodness and love.

This reminds me, too, of the time someone left a human turd on the floor of my friend's room. I have no idea why this happened, but I guess Dan had made himself an enemy, and the enemy decided it would be fair to take a shit on Dan's bedroom floor. The school authorities, of course, were hardly amused, and they threatened to perform a "genetic test" to find out who had done this stupid thing. They said to all the students at our school assembly that the "genetic test" would let them know exactly who had shat on Dan's floor. They said that whoever had done it might as well fess up, to spare them the expense of the "genetic test", and if he fessed up, his punishment would be reduced. Interestingly, they never brought it up again, which we, the general student population, took to mean that some idiot had bought the whole "genetic test" thing and decided to step forward as the perpetrator of this shitty misdeed. I asked Dan, but he said he wasn't allowed to talk about it. To this day, I don't know who did it. At least it wasn't my floor. This is what you can expect from sending your kids to fancy boarding schools.

All this could be different. But who can tally the cost? Cartoon spinach. I see the emblems of others. Terrified doesn't cut it. You have to be vicious if you want to know what these people are thinking. They stare at you with not even suspicion, not even that. Their self-loathing is all-consuming.

Disgust, you see? Does it not make you want to weep? Sometimes I wonder why there are no dogs left in this world. What happened to them? I will tell you my theory now. It is my theory that there are only dogs left, and some of us have lost even the basic gist of things. Who doesn't want to be kicked into the corner? Who doesn't want to be neglected? I have not fed my dog in several months. And still he soldiers on. What choice does he have?

It is not in our nature to try not to live. In this red sack of flesh the heart will beat forever. Even beyond the constraints of death. There is no telling how long a single heart can beat, for no one has lived that long. Let us consider it a blessing. And let us be modest in our attire and in our work. Let us pray that someday the heart will beat in a manner visible to us. But until that day, let us prepare for the flood from which there is no escape.

When I listen to myself speaking to the butcher, or the

postman, I cannot help but hate the sound of my own voice. Why the cynicism? Why the despair? Why play the prophet, amid so many other prophets of greater standing? When someone says Good morning, is that not some incantation? Have you met a greater magician than the idiot who greets you at the door?

In any case, be very good to the neighbor. Be very good to the kitty. Be good to the children, the parents. Be good and be good and be good and be BIG!

Which brings me to the heart of the matter: DO NOT SUCCUMB TO THE PLEASURES OF SELF-RELIANCE. DO NOT BE DECEIVED BY THE PROMISE OF A LIFE WELL-LIVED. SURRENDER COMPLETELY TO THE DISAPPOINTMENT THAT HAS UNFOLDED AS YOUR LIFE FROM THE MOMENT IT BEGAN, AND WILL UNFOLD AS YOUR LIFE UNTIL THE VIOLENCE TOMORROW AND BEYOND HAS COMPLETELY SUBSIDED.

Seriously. Let this grand disappointment overwhelm you. If there is even a sliver of resistance, you have not understood what is coming, Martha. Worse, you are practicing a skill for which there is no use. Resist or don't but you will have no choice in the long run. And there is no short run, not really. That's what I meant about empires.

But this is not a sermon on the virtues of pessimism. Only an optimist can speak of the coming fires. It is beautiful to see God in the Devil and the Devil in your beloved. For then there is only one thing left to fear — the loss of that capacity, the cracking of those hard-earned spectacles.

See the Devil in everything. Trust me. When you see a flower, see the Devil in that. When you fall in love, love the Devil in that. When you see the Devil, do not be fooled, but see through that Devil, through to the Devil in that. See the Devil in your children, your parents, your bed. When you wake, greet the Devil. When you pray, pray to him.

And what will you discover, having conditioned yourself

thus? You will see that the Devil you see is nothing but the nullity of things. To see a flower and see God is just to see a flower. To see a flower and see the Devil is to see the way in which that flower presents as not a flower. That's it; the joke is told over and over until you get it.

See that many times. See it in sleep and in dreams. Prepare yourself.

And practice creating zero-space. This is the space of non-interference. Listen to me because this is important, this is the secret. I am telling you about the priests of tomorrow. When the bloody rain begins to pour you will remember my words and think yes, yes he was on to something.

THE TRUE PRIEST AS THE NEW FATHER

What is zero-space? It is the nothing-bubble that forms around the TRUE PRIEST, the SHAMAN OF THE VOID, and it is what every living creature seeks as a place of final rest. Enter this zero-space and the organism of you begins to relax. You become aware all at once of your great wish to die here, in this nothing-bubble. More surprising still, you see in a flash that you have always wanted only this, to die, to find this space which is null and mindless and weightless. All creatures seek their final bed from the moment of their inception. Life is nothing but the search for this true resting place. And that is what the zero-space is, and the TRUE PRIEST knows it.

When you sit before the SHAMAN OF THE VOID, his eyes contain you. Whatever you think or say, he absorbs it like a sponge and digests it for you. Though you cannot contain your own energetic ejaculations, the TRUE PRIEST dissolves everything for you. You feel it happening but do not know quite how it all works. You've entered the nothing-bubble generated by this remarkable being.

It is the mantra of the SHAMAN OF THE VOID, the TRUE PRIEST: I AM A DESTROYER. PEOPLE COME TO ME TO DIE.

Recite this mantra and you, too, may plant those karmic seeds.

Strive for nothing less than the cultivation of this great non-capacity. Before you can even begin, you must learn to detect zero-space in your experience, however vague it may be at first. More important still, learn to recognize those who gift the nothing-bubble to others, freely, anonymously. Then spend as much time as you can around them, for they will burn your stupidities away without telling you. They will never admit to it; in fact, incredible though it may seem, they may not even know that they are soaking in the zero-space.

71

Such a person is what Tomorrow's flood will teach us to worship. Little pockets of zero-space will form here and there, and the Shamans of the Void will be unprotected from the torrents of blood yet somehow...different.

To them the others will turn. In their despair, their absolute confusion, these broken, bleeding corpses will seek the space of dying, and will feel safe in the bubbles of nothing. Don't just take me at my word. Feel it in yourself, this drive to die in the correct place.

When the fire comes, you will know the zero-space as a field of kindness.

Do not say prepared or unprepared, for every particle of your life warns of the coming violence, and yet — who can prepare but by staying upright and tense?

Do not say unprepared. In this tension of training there is productive strain, growth, contraction, Christ-like purity of thought. So train away, practice. Practice all the way to the end, until the rain starts and you see that it is red and you could not possibly have prepared for this, not in the way you were preparing, not in any way. Yet if you can cultivate the zero-space, that is preparation for the fire.

Do not say prepared. Do not say ready. You're not. Damn you, Millie.

We must picture ourselves aflame, running through hell, seeking only the possibility of death. But hell is our immortalization. Who has not learned to die in life cannot die in death. All this talk of nothing-bubbles is retrospective. Don't think too hard about it. See us all streaking through the fields of hell with our hair on fire, and ask yourself, Under whose shadow could we feel safe to die under such circumstances?

Correct. And such a man must choose to become a TRUE PRIEST, a circle of death. That choice will ring across time and space, negating both. And the choice is made only by the recitation of this mantra: I AM A DESTROYER. PEOPLE COME

TO ME TO DIE.

Recite it again. Let it sink into your bones. Then travel across the world making it true. Do not harm a soul and do not become a vegetarian and never succumb to the temptations of being good or bad or both. Simply choose to see the Devil where others see only the quotidian. Look the Devil in the eye and he disappears. Always find the Devil and see him and see through him. Do this over and over. Here is a coffee mug, and here is the Devil — seen through. Here I see my woman, but I see the Devil too — seen through. The TRUE PRIEST, destroyer, to whom people go to die, sees through the Devil and from that seeing creates and sustains a field of zero-space. The animal in everyone can detect this, even if the human can't.

I AM A DESTROYER. PEOPLE COME TO ME TO DIE.

So let them come. But until they come, see through the Devil in everything you encounter. And when they come, see through the Devil in them.

An old story. Timelessly stupid. Blow me, Sam Folkes. We continue with the torpedo of self-aggrandizing dog. Still, sometimes…

Sometimes when I assemble my armies and launch into battle, I do not know my enemy because I do not know myself. A mistake as traditional as that of not knowing myself because I do not know my enemy. Still, the coming violence is the product of the first mistake, that of not knowing the enemy because I don't know myself. Everyone knows it's coming, but they think it's because they don't know themselves because they don't know their enemy. Wrong. If they knew themselves they would know their enemy, which, would you believe it, would turn out to be only the concept of an enemy. It could have gone either way. At previous moments in history, it has been different, to an extent but only to an extent, the balance shifts, there are only two possibilities and both lead to violence.

So am I fetishizing the end? But I didn't say the end is

coming. I said what everyone already knows, that tomorrow is the exceptional violence of sleep. This is not the End Times. There's no such thing. No, that's not the message we all can hear in our hearts. It is not that the end is coming, but that starting tomorrow, perhaps even tonight, the tilt toward violence will be definitive. False prophets will speak of the end, but true prophets will speak only of the zero-space. I am not calling myself a prophet, but you may choose to see me as one if you like. Aspire with me to the TRUE PRIESTHOOD. Let us nothing-bubble the shit out of the looming inferno.

Q: How can I make myself useful once the violence comes?

A: Be exceptional in your capacity for non-interference.

Q: How can I recognize a TRUE PRIEST?

A: You will know a TRUE PRIEST by the fear that abruptly melts in your lap as you creep closer. You will see at once that you want to die.

Q: What are the essential features of a TRUE PRIEST?

A: Zero-space follows him as a spherical field of non-reactivity. If there is no zero-space, there is no TRUE PRIEST. This is the first law. The TRUE PRIEST may be young or old, male or female. Skin color will not matter because we will all be skinless from the fire.

Q: What kind of language does the TRUE PRIEST use?

A: Words when necessary.

Q: What kind of companionship would a TRUE PRIEST seek?

A: Wolves and foxes make the best companions for the TRUE PRIEST. Both are reviled creatures. The TRUE PRIEST learns to befriend the wolf and the fox.

Q: Will there be false priests dancing around as TRUE PRIESTS?

A: Always. However, you will know them by the absence of the absence that is zero-space.

Q: Confusingly, you refer to zero-space as a field, yet also as an absence. It seems paradoxical in a not-good way.

A: That is correct. But the confusion vanishes once you step into the zero-space.

Q: Just to be perfectly clear, are zero-space and nothing-bubble exactly equivalent?

A: For all practical purposes, yes.

Q: Is there a subtle theoretical distinction to be made between them, though?

A: Not sure.

Q: What clothes must a TRUE PRIEST wear?

A: There will be no clothes, not even skin. We all shall wear flames when fire comes, and blood when rain comes. And if we find a TRUE PRIEST, our broken bodies shall be exposed in the golden wind.

Q: What is the place where there is no hot or cold?

A: Zero-space.

Q: Is a TRUE PRIEST a master?

A: All masters create this field of zero-space around them. Some have the capacity to energize that field. They set it ablaze with vibratory excellence. Orgasm. That is not neutral. Others turn the field into a masochistic bog, a soul-sucking voiding of the void. That is not neutral. The impact is real, but it is a sludging of rigidities. We don't want sludge. The zero-space is completely neutral, and this neutrality shreds the rigidities that enter into contact with it. This shredding is ultimate purification. The animal feels it and rejoices, the human notices it and dies. All masters are capable of generating zero-space around them, but do not forget that not all masters want the best for you. A TRUE PRIEST will keep the field of zero-space neutral, that is, properly zero. The masochistic bog is negative, a minus one. The vibratory excellence is positive, a plus one. The TRUE PRIEST knows the neutral.

Q: Neither sacred nor profane?

A: Neither Devil nor God.

Q: Yet you command us to see the Devil, to see through him.

You are specific about doing so with the Devil. Why not with God?

A: God is the positive aspect of what we see. We are conditioned to see God and respond to the Devil. So we shift things around, and see the Devil while responding to God. Again the concept of returning to zero-space. At other times in history we have seen too much Devil and responded to too much God. But if we cannot see the Devil in the everyday object, we are trapped by an unconscious desire to be good in a world that does not require it of us. If we see through the Devil, we are free to be good without good and evil.

Q: Again, though, you tell use not to succumb to the pleasures of a life well-lived. Isn't being free to be good a way of living well?

A: The problem is in trying to live well. It is a rejection of life itself.

Q: Is the TRUE PRIEST omniscient?

A: No. But he understands the difference between ignorance and stupidity.

Q: What is the difference between ignorance and stupidity?

A: Ignorance is relative. Stupidity is absolute. Ignorance we can correct with knowledge, experience, words. We can play with ignorance as we play with matter, sculpt it as we sculpt societies and identities. Through the scientific method we chop away at our ignorance; but stupidity remains and sustains this chopping away. Through religious practice we elevate our ignorance and attempt to purify it. Through the law, we try to protect ourselves from our ignorance. It is stupidity, though, that makes law simultaneously necessary and pointless. Stupidity is that element of ignorance that cannot be corrected, absolute ignorance. It is that veil through which we see a world we believe we recognize. Stupidity is the veil we rely on when we try to lift the veil. The wise ones are informed by their intuitive sense of this absolute stupidity. They have dropped some of the shackles of ignorance, but they are as stupid as anyone else. They accept, in an inarticulable way, the paradoxical interplay of ignorant and stupid. When they try to speak of it, they sound misanthropic. As though it were a problem to be drowning in stupidity. All of this, the coming violence will resolve.

Q: What is the first sign of progress on the journey to TRUE PRIESTHOOD?

A: It is a shift in our understanding of the question "How do I express the inexpressible?" The first phase of practice is, essentially, a drawn-out grappling with our sense that there is something "beyond" that needs to be expressed in some way. It feels inexpressible, even to ourselves. We are not even sure what we are fundamentally attached to, except on strictly intellectual terms. Abstract suffering, that general sense of dissatisfaction that can't be pinpointed, feels tied up with this "beyond" but whether it's as the other side of the coin or the same side isn't clear. And by focusing on this "beyond" that we cannot even locate, we inadvertently end up focusing on our own suffering. This can take many guises. "I must rediscover the inner peace I have lost" or "I must locate the source of my sense of self" or "My insight needs to be validated by someone else who knows". (In Lacanian terms, it's as if we were trying to prove to ourselves that the other does not exist, in a way that would seem convincing to another. Or like asking our testicles to confirm that we are not castrated. It is more than a simple misunderstanding, but it's nothing other than a simple misunderstanding.) Then the shift occurs. At that point, the sense of the "beyond" may still be present, but it's deeply incorporated into "here". Instead of desperately trying to express the "inexpressible" that we were looking for, more and more we feel driven to express our knowledge of the inexpressible as what we actually are. And the need to express this inexpressibility is a defining feature of the long process of the integration of insight. The present moment is more readily present. The question is whether we can stop getting in the way of life as an ongoing expression of what we had previously found inexpressible. Speaking of "life" in these terms feels less phony and precious than it used to, and more technically accurate. And then, even that shifts. The worry about the inexpressible, while in a way more vivid and discernible in every moment than ever, loses its hold on the moment. Here it becomes very easy to notice suffering everywhere as just a play of illusions. The question "How do I express the inexpressible?" is both answered and unanswerable at the very same moment in the three times.

Q: By what mark shall I judge the TRUE PRIEST's relationship to truth?

A: There are those who see the truth and speak it, and those who hear the truth and repeat it. The TRUE PRIEST is silent about the truth, but in his presence the truth is felt as a longing for death.

Q: Are there any TRUE PRIESTS operating today?

A: Some years ago, this fellow Turtle McDurdle (real name) tried to squeeze some life out of the thing. Didn't work. Total disaster. That's what happens, what always will happen, when you lack the vision needed. The thing's not to be squeezed. Any squeezing by a non-professional is going to go wrong. And the professionals don't have the moral courage to squeeze it right either. So who squeezes?

Turtle McDurdle used to say the life of the thing was in the squeezing of it. So to be clear, this is a literal squeezing we're on about. Squeeze the life out of the thing, with your bare hands. That's how Turtle saw it, and how he said it. But squeeze as he might, he couldn't do it. Just the idea of squeezing the life out of something. Just that. Fucking idiots, but there you go, that's who we call entrepreneurs these days.

Anyway, what Turtle did next was to try his hand as something a little more ambitious but also, bizarrely, more attainable. He got curious about zero-space. He felt it, he felt himself abruptly dying in the presence of a stranger. With his hippie friends, he'd have said it was something about the stranger's energy. Something vibrational. But it was better and different. The stranger's eyes emptied Turtle right out. Within a few seconds of contact with the stranger, Turtle could feel his own organism collapsing in the zero-space. Every particle of death in him came alive.

The stranger said nothing and moved on. Turtle contracted back into himself. But the longing to die never went underground again.

Be like Turtle, who saw the feebleness of his insight into reality and changed his name legally to Turd Dull McDurrrr Dull. Friends started calling him McDurrrr. His wife Rebecca called him M'dear McDurrrr. McDurrrr got pissy if you left out an R.

But be like him, like McDurrrr. who resolved to cultivate some of that zero-space for himself. He knew in his bones, which is where it matters, that you gotta be a TRUE PRIEST or no priest at all. And the problem is we're all potential priests, and that potential gnaws at us as we go around being tormented people. McDurrrr withdrew from society and his marriage for three years, and moved to Togo. There he pursued deep purification of spirit and, more difficult, of body. When he returned, having attained some measure of liberation from the violence of sleep, his wife had remarried (illegal, because they'd never divorced — ILLEGAL), and his former friends shunned him, for they could sense the death around him, the small but hard-won field of zero-space he projected. They felt threatened. He could awaken their desire for death but did not yet have the experience and the mystical capacity to contain that desire on their behalf and permit their organisms to perish.

Still, let us commend McDurrrr.

When the violence comes, those like McDurrrr will have prepared, and failed to prepare, in just the right way. They will be no better off in absolute terms, but on a relative level they will embody the absolute for those stuck in the relative. For the sake of their fellow idiots, TRUE PRIESTs like McDurrrr bandy about words like absolute and relative, if they speak at all. This talk of absolute and relative, real and apparent, true and conditional, intrigued a young man calling himself Guantanamo Jones. That wasn't his real name, of course. His real name was Guantanamo John. But you can understand his not wanting to be associated with other Johns. This young man became McDurrrr's first and only disciple. As McDurrrr's capacities as a mystic of the nothing-bubble grew, so too did his confidence as a transmitter of these mysterious teachings. In Guantanamo Jones, McDurrrr saw a future TRUE PRIEST. So they began working together.

Let's reiterate, however, that you can be neither prepared nor unprepared for the coming violence. The slumbering cosmos awakens tomorrow, and the fires and floods will be nothing but the movements of its eyelids opening. Ask your expert forecasters how best to prepare for the catastrophe of the great slumber's conclusion.

A TRUE PRIEST today does everything he can to WAKE UP, WAKE UP, FOR THE FLOOD IS COMING. But a TRUE PRIEST tomorrow knows he is only as awake as a flea. The eyelash may be close to the eye, but it cannot see. McDurrrr was pleased to see that Guantanamo Jones understood this, only peripherally at first, but the insight was there.

Arduous training led to a deepening of insight. Guantanamo Jones could no longer relate in any way to his old self, and changed his name to Long Time Ago Jones. McDurrrr took to calling him Time Ago. This later became Tim Ago, which was easier socially. Finally, they settled on Tim McGee, a properly human name, though he spelled it Tim McGeeee in honor of his master, McDurrrr.

McDurrrr and McGeeee were the first two Patriarchs in a lineage you've never heard of. Starting tomorrow, or perhaps tonight, when the extraordinary violence erupts, you will seek people like them out. No other death will do.

And now, listen to me very carefully. Something big is about to happen in the next hour. I think you may want to pay attention to what's going on around you. First, may I suggest you take a look at the visual field? Just stare at it for a moment. See what I mean? Something is off. What is it? Could be that what your eyes are picking up doesn't match what your brain is showing you? Could be that you are not seeing what you're seeing, but seeing what you are not seeing? Think about that. It will blow your mind.

Now, it is certainly true that you are being fucked with. You're being fucked by everyone you know. Like me, like Tim McGeeee, you see little things. Gorilla. Godzilla. The giant eight of slumber, the giant slumber of eight. Though there is nothing special about that number. Every number sleeps. Unlike the cosmos, mathematics must remain insentient. It is the superstructure, the understructure, the underlying cosmic reality that cannot possibly awaken. Mathematics is what ultimately you have seen today. Behold the mathematical. See the Devil in it. See through the Devil in basic algebra. It will heal your heart.

Do not sing hallelujah just yet.

Behold that which is visual. Take the visual into the eye and project it outward into the blissful void that is all you see. Become the void of seeing itself and transcend even that, until the devil cannot even be seen through but only apprehended as some sort of joke.

And listen to what is listening to you, and in that loop become the visual again. Trust that this is possible, that these are not mere words, and no simple incantation could ever take you where I am taking you now. This is more than hypnosis, more than domination. I am revealing to you what you can reveal to any bird. Like St Francis, preaching to all of God's creatures, you can be the Machiavelli of the soul. Do not be fooled by the glamour, do not be seduced by the wealth in heaven, but stay exactly where you are and stick your fat fuck face in the muzzle of silent observation.

When the violence comes it will strip from you all that you have gathered as yourself. Either you will seek out a priest or you will become one. In either case, still you must burn with everyone else. But should you choose the mantle of the TRUE PRIEST, SHAMAN OF THE VOID, container and sustainer of the zero-space, you will be all that remains of kindness in the world to come.

You will lose what you love, what you hate, what you cherish, what you celebrate, what you revile, what you despise. You will lose the people you never thought you could lose, as well as those you always considered expendable. You will see on the faces of those you love only horror, desperation, repentance and the precious desire for death. The organism of each man shall drive his mind to recognize around the TRUE PRIEST a field of death. The organism always knows. The organism thrives on chaos. It is the organism that loathes what the mind insists upon. But how can the organism thrive on chaos, you ask. Surely chaos is exactly what the organism cannot withstand. Precisely so. If you have not yet understood that all the organism seeks is a place to die, you have understood nothing. Let this be a warning to those who think they can grok it in one go. If you think you understand, that too is a protection against death. Let it go, but do not force the letting go or you are back in the world of trying to stay alive.

What a paradox, a paradox indeed. With every breath, your body keeps you alive. The organism's every pulsation and twitch keeps it going, and yet the whole process is nothing but a quest to stop the pulsations and the twitches. What kind of Creator God are we dealing with? I will show you when the violence comes.

If I were a male porn actor I would take great pleasure in

calling myself a working stiff.

Do not think me an irreligious man. We cannot escape religion. Our DNA is organized according to religious logic. The double helix is but two snakes that dangle as the penis of Satan. And God put that penis there. I worship Satan as I worship you. I worship you as I worship God.

Scream that it is fabulous. Let everybody hear you. Scream to all that the serpentine double helix dangling as the penis of Satan is all part of the plan. Simultaneously you must let go of all notions of plan, of cosmic design, for there is nothing but torment in the layer directly above the mathematical. If you can understand this, let go of that understanding, too, for there is an evil lesson here.

The double helix is the source of the Lord's joy. The Lord's joy is ours. Weather is rename the double helix the Double Felix. We are doubly happy in the presence of the dangling penis.

I had a psychiatrist examine this document as part of our ongoing attempt to diagnose me as something other than schizophrenic. He was well pleased by my articulate description of the nature of reality. He revoked my license to practice as a schizophrenic. He declared me fully healed.

Well, how would you diagnose me? Am I a prophet, a madman or a charlatan?

My father told me that the only way to be happy is to see through the Devil in all things. This is back when I was very young, way too young to form reliable memories. And yet I remember it clearly, for some part of me is ageless and deathless. As is some part of you, I might add. Where can this immortal aspect of the self be located? I shall tell you. In the nothing-bubble.

Seek out a worthy priest and die immediately. Do not hesitate. Do this as soon as possible, ideally before nightfall.

St Augustine gets to spend five hundred pages whining about the dreadful implications of stealing pears. Why can't I

steal pears and whine about how awful I am? You know why
this matters? You know why we spend 500 pages talking about
stealing pears? Because it's the details. That's where you find
your soul, that's where you learn there is no other way to be but
enmeshed in detail. The person is in the details, the details are
lost in other details, there's nothing but implication and subtlety
no matter how hard you try to bring it all back to some grand
simple point of reference. You can't do it, McGeeee. You can't
point at something and say that's the point right there, that's
what my life is all about. It's all shades and caveats and endless
pursuits of increasingly esoteric objects that dissolve into even
tinier pieces of sand when you grasp them.

Q: Can you express this less cryptically?

A: Yes. Though I proclaimed great love, I found in me the
cold wet shaking terror of the sea, and I was humbled, and
much aggrieved. I sought to break that subtle curse whereby the
inconceivable thousand raised to the power of six is trapped in
a quintillion — and was revealed a muddy meddling forger of
an intuitive impersonal complexity of which the carnival of self
cannot partake.

Q: Whoa, did you hear that??

A: What?

Q: Listen... It sounds like my time...is being WASTED.

A: Oh no, dear fellow. This is not all a waste of time. We have
only a few hours left before everything turns to chaos. This is the
only home. Here is where all homes begin and end. Here there is
no outside of home, and no inside.

See your hands. At first you see them but do not see them.

To inhabit the body of here. Discarding all discardables.
Discarding by forgetting; forgetting by discarding. To be here
as the here itself, to be the room and that contained therein. To
touch this here by remembering this here, grasping it with the
fiercest attention, and relaxing into that grasping. That is the
body of this place, the body into which you step. This table never

ends. The windows are infinitely distant. The pressure of sitting cannot be forgotten when you welcome it. Who welcomes what? The welcoming, too, is discarded, an amusing formality. Even the recognition of the present becomes formality, posturing. Always returning to the place you did not leave to claim the only body until it is forgotten.

Looking soberly upon my life until now, I see that much of it has been spent desperate to end the desperation, miserable about the misery, confused about the confusion. I have seen the logic at work here. I have tried too hard to stop trying, spent too long unhappy about my own unhappiness, wasted too much trying not to waste. When I think, my thinking propels my body forward, tightens the world around me, removes something beautiful from the very stuff with which thinking keeps itself fed: the world around me. I find myself paying less and less attention to the barest, most immediately accessible things. I do not notice what it feels like to be in my own body.

WHEN YOU CANNOT FIND A TRUE PRIEST, everything that should feel normal feels a little too important, mildly threatening, worth keeping an eye on. Going outdoors should feel normal to the extent that it should *not* feel abnormal; sitting on your couch reading a book should feel normal because it is a perfectly normal thing to do. But something about leaving the house or just sitting down reading *does* feel wrong: you cannot focus on walking into the elevator and pressing the button and just being in the elevator because you are busy focusing on twenty other things: not just your appearance in the mirror (you look ill, your coat is wrong, your stubble screams pervert) but your body, the ongoing arguments in your mind, the feeling that you will get in trouble, or that you will be noticed by the wrong person, or that the uncomfortable sensation in your sock will become unbearable if you don't adjust it before you step out of the elevator. Everything's a threat. No aspect of this threatening world is terrible in itself, but it all goes into the mess that becomes your daily experience.

YOUR ORGANISM WISHES TO DIE.

Abnormal, then, becomes normal. In the abstract, there's no difficulty conjuring up an image of what this should all feel like: think of the quiet, smiling woman at the park the other day, who seemed so at peace, so unperturbed, so happy to be where she was doing no more than that, probably not worrying about the pebble in her shoe or the sweat stains under her arms or whether she's forgotten to reply to fifteen important emails. In this abstract understanding of what it is to be calm and free from anxiety, every aspect of the definition makes sense only in the negative: instead of being nervous, I am *not* nervous, and instead of fidgeting, I am able to *stop* fidgeting. I can sleep soundly instead of waking up at four in the morning worrying about something. The anxious mind's idea of "normal" itself an excruciatingly anxious idea, an obsessive idea: I'll be normal when I stop doing this, and this, and that, and I'd be better off if I could just get over this and this and this, but what's getting in my way is… this and that and… and that is why I am not normal.

THE ORGANISM SEEKS DEATH.

Sometimes I feel as though I were headed toward some magnificent religious conversion. Some mysterious shift into freedom. There has been a hell of a buildup: years of agonizing over trifles, wrestling with doubt, unshakeable guilt, inexpressible insecurity. I have had phases of knowing I take everything for granted in the most impotent way, and stretches of comical obliviousness to my good fortune. For seven decades I have felt the terror of a perfectly ordinary life, and longed for something radical, something utterly transformative that would make sense of things. I have felt that I needed an excuse, or someone's permission, to be charitable. I have wanted permission simply to exist, knowing nobody could grant me that comfort. The world has had no trouble forcing me to confront my own powerlessness, and, paradoxically, it has done it by showing me how seldom I choose to take matters into my own hands, how free I am. Being here is dizzyingly banal, and I have had a sense of my rootlessness since I can remember.

WHEN THE MIND BECOMES LIKE THIS, SEEK A TRUE PRIEST AND STEP INTO THE NOTHING-BUBBLE.

Q: And how can I summon a TRUE PRIEST?

A: There is a preliminary ritual. Cherish this most secret teaching and SEAL YOUR LIPS, LEST YOU INCUR THE WRATH OF CHRIST, YOU CUNT. Begin by physically relaxing the Body. Get a sense of your body as a whole. Identify any areas of tension that are obvious. Start by relaxing those. Time it with the out breath, so that every time you exhale you are allowing your body to return to a state of relaxation. Some particular things to look out for are: Tension in the pelvis and the buttocks that might be contributing to a sense of withholding and ungroundedness. Also the rib cage. It can be difficult to appreciate that there is a lot of tension there between individual ribs, in the intercostal muscles themselves. As you exhale, notice the tension between the ribs. Just exhale them away, all those little patterns of tension. In the shoulder blades, let them loosen up. The muscles of the back of the head, the neck. Particularly around the bump in the back of the head. You can choose to artificially tense it up, just a little bit, so that you can notice what it is that gets tense there. As you exhale that tension away, it is like the back of your head is slightly reaching for the ceiling. One thing you can do is feel the cushion or the chair under you and then at the same time feel the muscles in the back of your head so that you are holding those two things simultaneously, which can create a sense of bodily integrity. Two things which seem far apart are suddenly held together.

Now focus specifically on facial tension. There is a huge amount of unconscious tension in the little muscles around the eyes and the cheeks, the forehead and the earlobes. So, be very meticulous in looking for tension there. The more softly you look for tension, the more obvious the tension will become. The jaw, the tongue itself is tense. And now focus especially on the eyes, the eyes themselves, the eyeballs have tension in them. Let them relax and in particular, feel the back of the eyes. Feel the tension in the back part of your eyeballs, closest to your brain. And you can hold that along with the muscles in the back of your head to create a complete feeling of the head as a whole organism unto itself.

And now let's open up the gaze. Your eyes are open and very soft, unfocused, passively receiving light and color, and holding the edges of your vision all at once even if it is blurry. It doesn't matter what you're seeing. You don't need to focus or be clear on what is arising visually. The point is to allow visual experience to emerge exactly as it is. You don't need to interfere with your vision, which means you don't have to interpret it. If it is blurry, you don't have to make it sharp. You just let the visual field arise softly and vividly and silently, until it is relatively stable, and the periphery of your vision is easy to hold along with what is right in front of you. Having opened up the visual field, return to the space just behind the eyes where there is very subtle tension. From here you can look out at the visual field and merge the face with the visual field as though they were happening in the same space. It is like you are seeing your own face because all of the muscles in your face are included in the visual field. Hold these two fields simultaneously until they feel like a single field of unified experience. At this point, be clear about how much effort you are making, because all that you need is ten percent of your maximum effort. One out of ten is all you need here because the more effort you make, the more you end up artificially separating these fields, segmenting them into a somatic field and a visual field. Efforting separates the senses. And so for this part of setting up this open space, you need to be clear that you are aiming for gross non-doing. Gross doing is actively trying and actively tensing up, maybe without noticing.

Gross non-doing is deliberately choosing to let that tension go. Let the fields merge as they have been all along: never making more than ten percent of your maximum effort to hold these two fields together ongoingly and softly. Now at this point it can be helpful to loosen the sense of the body's solidity by taking the sensations of your body, and particularly the rising and falling of the breath, and making them cloudlike rather than bodylike so the movement in your body as you breathe is the gentle billowing of a very, very soft, thin cloud that is spreading out into the room, into the visual field, slowly. The goal here is not so much that you visualize an actual cloud, because that will reintroduce efforting. The point is to see that you can treat your somatic experience as cloudlike, soft, thin, and silently spreading outward instead of contracting inward.

Deepen your access to this spacious, empty field that you are cultivating gently. As you inhale you can take the perspective that you are breathing in from the visual field, that the air is coming from the visual field and that is where it returns when you breathe out. And the same goes for the muscular tension, as you exhale, whatever tension you're building up you release back into this empty field full of light and color. Experience is the world's slowest dance.

Now, holding this visual field that is merged with the somatic field, you can include the other senses. For example, if you have a constant ringing in your ears or if there is a background sound that seems continuous over time; it may be the wind; it may be rain; it may be the air conditioning; it may be a train in the distance; you can interpret that sound as if it is happening in this same field of unified experience. Gently, it is like you are seeing or feeling the sound. Make sure you haven't lost access to the muscles of your face and remember you are not looking at an external world. You are simply looking at your own face. The world is staring right back at you. No inside and no outside. And within this unusual space that doesn't really feel like normal space, there is something very present, timeless. Although your sensory experience is the world's slowest dance, there does seem to be something that is absolutely still and unreactive, silent and timeless. The more you can detect this gentle dance of experience, the more deeply you are truly resting in something timeless, the absolute now of this. You can intentionally recall a memory from the past or imagine something about the future but do so within this field and see what happens. Without losing sight of this endless moment, bring up the past or create the future and notice that it is happening in this totally persistent, absolute now that is timeless. Really allow that aspect of experience to emerge, to reveal itself. And here we enter the realm of subtle non-doing.

Gross non-doing is about choosing to relax, to make less effort and to allow the sensory fields to merge as they have been trying to do all along. Subtle non-doing is about bringing the level of effort from ten percent to one percent. And you do this by fully surrendering. You do not exclude anything. You attain gross non-doing by letting go, letting go of tension. And you attain subtle non-doing by letting in your thoughts, letting in your effort, letting in the sense of a separate witness, letting in the sense of the controller, until you can be very, very clear that there is some subtle part of you that keeps trying to interfere, to evaluate your experience in the background. Even if you can detect it, it will immediately generate a thought like: "Oh yeah, I'm trying to control this," which will then become another attempt to control this process. So just keep noticing the game at this very subtle level of interference. It is an energetic thing, the energy of interference. The subtlest agenda. You can't get rid of it. You just have to see it as the fastest dancer in this very slow dance included, so that now you have gross non-doing and subtle non-doing in a spaceless, timeless, unified, cloudlike, extremely soft, brilliantly aware moment of absolute newness. And all you do is hold this sense of general awareness as though you were staring back at your own face.

Practice until you can detect this energy of interference, moment by moment. Even looking for the energy of interference is interference. Gross non-doing is about letting go and subtle non-doing is about letting in. And the final piece is to make sure that you are available. Are you being available to your own experience? The sense of openhearted availability, which, once you can tune into, shows you another favorite strategy for hiding out. When you really let yourself be fully present and available as though someone you deeply cared about had just called your name and you were available, you can see that. You will realize the slightly healing quality of experience. When experienced in this way, reality has a slight tilt toward healing, and that is pleasant. So, the more available you are to this face of yours that is right in front of you, staring back at you, the more you can allow pleasure to saturate your experience. It is a silent, soft pleasure without narcissism, built into the fabric of your experience.

And from this point on you just leave yourself alone. Do this long enough and you will BREAK THAT SUBTLE CURSE WHEREBY THE INCONCEIVABLE THOUSAND RAISED TO THE POWER OF SIX IS TRAPPED IN A QUINTILLION.

HYPOTHESIS 0

Now, Martha, SISTER MINE, you would think that God would find a suitable convert in a character like me, but the religious epiphany has never happened. I've never, for example, found myself blinded while crossing the street, perhaps by the reflection of the sun in a bus window, and been seized by an intoxicating, all-encompassing love of everything around me that could only be explained by the presence of the divine. I've never discovered that foreign, but profoundly intimate, love burning in my blood (yes I have), and felt like giving everything to those around me and devoting my life to Christ, or to some equivalently respectable prophet. And while I've been reduced to uncontrollable sobs of gratitude and awe in the mountains, I never went back home thinking I'd found God (bullshit).

I guess I have simply not seen that light. And pathetically, I've sought it. I have sought this trip to peace, Martha, that path to solace, seven guaranteed ways of connecting to God. Those early nights, when I was seven or eight, spent staring into the dark ceiling above me wondering if God could read my mind never went away completely: they changed, in my teenage rebellion, into a hatred of smaller, failed gods, a fear of adult men who seemed to want to dominate me, fraudulent fathers. But the preoccupation with God, though inverted and focused on my failure to find a good reason to believe, was as strong as ever. It became a reverential fear of my own unconscious when I started reading Freud. Then it changed into a cocky belief that language, mere words, had served as the basis of whole civilizations, and that all meaning was an arbitrary human projection disguised as something natural, nature itself, inside the language of everyday discourse — the glorious undergraduate years. From there, my preoccupation with God, with meaning, shifted subtly into a smugly defeated, cynical appreciation of human folly. I could see patterns in the ways human beings were stupid, just as other wise men had done before me, so that simple rules of thumb were elevated to golden rules: if in doubt, assume someone just wants to be loved; always assume you don't know everything because you don't, and that way people won't find you intolerable; women do not want you to be too nice to them, but that's no excuse to be an unrepentant dick either, and anyway, men are the same; never expect others to be as grateful as you'd like them to be; also, people are listening to you with their own ears, not yours.

This was all my search for God, my search for something stable, some kind of truth, even if it meant finally paring my infinitely complex experience down to as dull an observation as: There is no ultimate truth. God himself must wrestle with this, so don't ask him for help.

Is there something absurd about wondering why your magical religious conversion has been so unfairly delayed? Can we imagine Saul on the road to Damascus, blinded by heavenly light, kneeling before a figure who squeals with delight, "It's me, Saul, Jesus, whom you have impatiently expected all this time!"?

And yet — though I never found God in a crazy religious frenzy, I have had frenzies of a sort, glimpses into that other dimension, one which isn't even there.

Very deep down, so artfully hidden away that I've often fooled myself about having overcome it, there is shame. It sits at my core, pernicious and masked. I do not know how it formed, and have only educated guesses about its role in my life, its effect on the slightest decisions. Often I forget that I am behaving, not out of educated conviction or sincerity or mere curiosity, but out of shame, and those are the times I most despise in hindsight. Though I cringe with shame to admit it, my greatest enemies have been people foolish enough to say something, whatever, that ignited my shame. I am *always* trying to protect myself from my own shame, and if I don't loudly declare its presence, I'll spend every word I write avoiding the topic entirely.

Ah, to hell with it, I see myself crying out faintly, see me naked first, then I'll tell you my name. That was not a good sentence. Already the doubt kicks in. I'm not proud of myself, and I worry that I'll be accused of exhibitionism, but if I give in to the worry, I give in to the shame, and I want to speak the shame out of hiding.

A pill will fix it.

HYPOTHESIS 1

You can measure time by the number of pills you can swallow at once.

It used to be one pill, one gulp of water. Every morning, before brushing your teeth, the one pill. That made you drowsy, so you switched to taking it in the evenings, as the doctor suggested. But that made sleep an uncomfortable mess of disjointed sensations, so you went back to mornings.

It would be hard not to focus on the shape of the pill. Its edges pushing against the tongue, then scraping very gently against the back of the throat. At the unpracticed stage, the pill could start dissolving in your mouth before you'd managed to swallow. It had a bitter, miserable chalky taste and made the ordeal of swallowing even harder. Then when you finally gulped the fucker down, the taste would linger as though you'd failed, as though even getting a little pill down was too difficult to do right.

The advice was to swallow with a small gulp of water, but by the time the daily dose had been increased to two pills — and later, to four pills, eventually simplified into two more powerful pills — such advice became annoying. Taking two gulps when one would do seemed a better idea: you were in a rush, out somewhere, or you just *felt* rushed, wanted to get it all over with. So there would be two pills sitting on the tongue, and a single gulp would dispose of both. At the unpracticed stage here, too, the pills would start dissolving before you could get them down, but soon it was easy to take three pills at once, then four, five or six, and then it wasn't a matter of how many pills you could swallow at once, but how quickly you could swallow all the pills you had to take that day so you could get on with more important things. Then you started playing around, showing off your ability to swallow twenty fish oil pills at once while also chewing gum.

When sickness of the soul becomes a problem of mental health, it starts a fascinating game. You must discover the rules after consenting to play; for there is no informed consent when it comes to having the insanity medicated out of you. You just don't know what the pills will do, what your role will be as the story of your mental health progresses, and which among your many masks will emerge as real at the end of the whole thing. What will become of the person you are desperately trying to save, the person you think you ought to be — someone a little happier than you, someone you remember smiling more than you do, whose problems were your problems but just didn't seem as overwhelming as they do today? None of these questions has an answer. Deep down, or far at the back of your mind, you know they are meaningless. But it would be too painful to say so. You take the pills. You learn to give yourself up slowly.

Still, as dramatic as it all sounds, like any play, it is just that — it is *play*. After the first prescription runs out, it is easier to get the second. There is a sense that the rules of the game are defining themselves, and it turns out you're pretty good at it. Life on medication, you discover, is just a series of tiny conditioning exercises. The more efficiently you can take your pills, the less you dwell on the act of taking them. They're barely even there. Eventually there's nothing separating you from the pill's effects, no bitter taste, no uncomfortable edge sticking in your throat or the worry that the pill is too big to swallow in one gulp. No gagging. No more frantically double-checking when you suspect you distractedly took your medication twice. You learn to travel with your pills. You plan a trip keeping in mind the amount of medication you have left before you've got to get more. You worry, as you make your way to the airport, whether the man scanning your bag will consider the amount of pills you're traveling with a little odd, and ask you about it. You feel that your ever-falling sex drive needs explaining, and part of your presentation of yourself to those you'd like to fuck involves making them understand that it's not that you don't find them attractive. It's just these fucking *pills*. They make sex less interesting somehow. (The doctor can recommend and prescribe Viagra or Cialis, by the way. It is an option he's happy to consider, he says, and it may well solve the problem, and he'd like you to feel things as intensely as before. Etcetera. Then you can go home and fall in love with her all over again. No? Okay, well, if the problem continues, you'll let the doctor know, yes?)

This material side of the medicated life — the gagging, the worrying, the planning — is where the resistance goes on most dramatically when you start taking the pills. It's where you learn your other stubborn and contradictory opinion on the matter: your body wants to push it all away, refuses to find the act of swallowing medication comfortable, and this affects you emotionally too. You get a little embarrassed, or you try to conceal the pill you're taking when staying over at someone else's house, because you've learned that people are unduly curious and will ask. When a friend says his brother's now on antidepressants, you wait to learn how your friend feels about it before telling him you take antidepressants, too, (and also antipsychotics, but one thing at a time here). It's likely that, at some point, everyone who needs to know about your mental health *condition* will know, and things will be less tinged with shame. Until then, it is all resistance, social and physical.

But take that resistance away, with its many moments of discomfort, and the rest resolves itself very neatly. And anyway, it's just a game. Perhaps you're buying into it more and more, and losing confidence in the magic, growing desperate, feeling your power vanish into the abyss — but the rules are clear. If you're not feeling better, maybe you need a higher dose. Take it to the big leagues, go harder. There is a specific dose that will be just right for you — it's all about finding it.

Your body becomes a total stranger. Feeling feelings feels

weird. Then it just feels wrong.

Over time, the distinctions you make will be between emotional states only, not between the physical and the emotional. You feel good on and between pills, and the pills themselves do not enter your awareness nearly as much. There is only so much the memory can do before the mind adapts to this new reality, and you start to convince yourself that you *are* this person on medication, and that life was not so different back then. You just used to be a person who needed medication and didn't have any, and now you're a person taking medication. The memories of life before pills, a year ago, five years ago, feel oddly naive, as though you can't believe you once thought you could solve your problems differently. When you are sufficiently broken in, it becomes not just possible but easy to condescend to your former, unmedicated self. You were so naive.

Like the smoker who only remembers he smokes when he notices he's down to two or three in a pack of twenty cigarettes, the medicated man only remembers the physical thingness of what he is, and the materiality of his cure, when he's about to run out of pills.

What will it take to wake up? How, in this daze, do you look into the big unblinking eye of your life?

Years later, long after you have overcome all this, and submitted to the unimaginable beauty of life, your uncle tells you that he remembers you, the protagonist of this unresolvable non-narrative, as a quiet, sullen, intense, zombie-like kid, slouching at the dinner table, drooling into his soup.

"No, literally. You were *drooling* into your soup," your uncle adds, not smiling, arching his eyebrows.

Drooling. Someone can, with impeccable honesty, say they remember you *drooling* into your soup, rendered near-vegetative by antidepressant and antipsychotic pills, and a lot of Valium.

HYPOTHESIS 2

The line between suffering and the perfection of every moment is both infinitesimally small and inconceivably great.

This, McGeeee, is the story of my profoundly miserable life, a life that has turned out to be absolutely, unbelievably, incommunicably perfect, a violent and horrible and ecstatic masterpiece, and very boring.

The misery of my life was one ongoing adventure of struggling to stop struggling, an addiction to shaming myself for being addicted to shaming myself for my addiction to shame. I have lived a life of unbelievable material privilege, and devoted almost all of it to breaking out of bind after bind, escaping from this endless discomfort in my own body and soul. I have been hysterically terrified of life, traumatized by events that contained no real danger, humiliated by people who never meant to humiliate me. Imprisoned by my fear of imprisonment.

And I swear to you, McGeeee, who wanders this world in a situation close to mine, that I have found freedom. A freedom more perfect than I can possibly express in words. I have seen the absolute perfection of every single thing. I SEE IT NOW.

I've seen the sunlight on the rocks. The wasp on my shoulder and the gushing of the stream: they are perfect. Perfect, enduring, speechless love flowing in and out of every crack on every wall of every house in the world. As a lifelong agnostic, I am relieved not to have to mention God. Just this amazing process that is unfolding all around us, pissing off those who, like me, would have liked to believe that life is only pain and suffering. Where there is zero, there is impending life.

Like an earlier incarnation of McGeeee, another emanation of the zero-space, this once-McGeeee whose eyes were wide open took in every crack in every surface of every thing. He could see details in things without trying: the wrinkles in his pillow were as deep and intricately created as the whole of his inner life. None of that habitual dread of getting out of bed and into clothes and into the foreign land of being himself haha — nothing of the kind. Nothing was wrong that morning; nothing worried him, no one angered him.

But don't you get it yet, you sick son of a bitch, you whiny self-pitying fuck, or don't you want to get it, is this too much for your brain to take. It's really very simple. This is pain, old pal, simple, brute life, everything you have, right now, pain. You can feel it in your chest but you will deny it to yourself over and over and over and. It's like a bear trap has gone off in your chest, like your chest *is* a bear trap that has gone off in the bear trap of your chest, the whole chest feels so tight it's like a balloon being rubbed with a wet cold hand, that same feeling, like chewing on a dry towel, like your mind is chewing the dry towel of your body.

YOU, DEAR SISTER, will need to understand this on my behalf.

The SELF is a PERCEPTUAL ILLUSION.

The EGO is a PERPETUAL DELUSION.

IN THE ZERO-SPACE

Because back then, Mildred, I never wondered: Will I think back to this? Will I miss the sand and the water? I knew I never would. I thought, sitting there with you, that my nostalgia would be exceptional: that I'd recall other details, the light reflecting off some surface I alone had the soul to notice, or how a gull took a clever swerve from one side of the sky to another as if to show me, and me alone, that the universe worked cleverly, artistically.

You would be a memory of a good summer, I thought, a summer I knew then belonged to my youth. I exploited my youth. I knew, and you knew with me in your way, how someone older and sadder would tell us to seize this now, for life, in principle, was going to be very long but this part went too fast. Seize it, an older man would say, had said to me, in different voices and places. This, *now*, take what you have and be young. You have her, have her now. Nothing you do now will matter unless you fail to do it. Hold on to nothing but do it all exquisitely.

And I knew anything we did might be excused that way. I thought: everyone around is young, too, but I have heard the older people speak when they are sad. I have heard the regret implied in their advice. I am clever and I'm young. None of this will matter. Kiss her. Be cruel but earnest. I am clever and I have the youth that grants me endless pardons.

So I seized the immortality I thought I was too clever to believe in, just as you seized yours. Casual, unconvinced by each other, but desperate to convince in our turn, we did flippancy, we tried needing nothing in the world but what we saw before us. We seized what seized us. And that night it was the sea we had, and the sand, the distant chanting of hippies we did not think meant what they did. It was a calf and its reticent mother lowing quietly under one of the cabins built into the trees.

I don't recall the clever swerving of a gull, or the refraction of stray light through some crack in the waves. Nothing brilliant about me comes to mind from those days. You were fascinating, but perhaps more now, now my distracting brilliance has stopped blinding me, now that I can hear what I think I remember you saying. We fought. I stood and shook the sand from my legs and said not to drag me into your hole. What did I mean? That you wished nothing more than to be stuck where you were, feeling what you felt. Perhaps I was too many things to be happy as your pain. But it lasted only hours. When I was asleep in our cabin, I felt you climb the stairs, felt you get onto your inch-thick mattress on your part of the floor. You knocked my head back against the wall. We knew how romantic, how young it all was, to reunite this way. We had spent our time apart before, we would spend it again once this was over. But how good we were at this awareness of doing youth right.

I am not much older now. I think ten years have passed since we met, perhaps eight since we last touched. The details that return are sea, sand, argument and lowing calf. Despite all our pretensions, we ended up a simple memory of something already vanishing then, half-extinguished by our cleverness.

I wish I'd known that knowing didn't matter then. I wish I'd filtered less through a future I never got. I wish I'd never thought there was a right way to be young.

But know this. In the nothing-bubble, even youth fucks right off. On the one hand, there is the illusion of DEATH: the misunderstanding of death as somehow opposed to life, a misunderstanding that has no basis in experience. This is an assumption that leads to behavior calculated to prevent death, which is called self. The minute the possibility of death emerges, its opposite is also created, namely life. Paradoxically, the fear of death generates the fear of life, and from there a false conception of life emerges that depends completely on a false conception of death.

On the other hand, the illusion of DEPTH: a misunderstanding of the relationship between the senses, a distinction between mind and body, self and other, inner and outer. Experience is constructed on the basis of a misperception of the senses as somehow cohering and representing "something" that has depth and external body. The inability to think purely superficially, without implicit reference to depth, is the underlying cause of all ensuing dualistic thought. And this is anterior to the illusion of death, a more basic mechanism.

It takes uncommon courage to confront the fact that we are utterly and pointlessly ruined by the activity of our own minds. And it takes exceptional wisdom to see how perfect that is.

When the violence comes, that perfection alone will soothe your mind as your organism succumbs to the zero-space's song. At that point, there is only you.

You, the embattled Buddha, sitting there, always here, looking who knows where into this mysterious ultimate real thing we others cannot see. Saying this is it, look no further, you must strive and strive and strive until you have stopped, and then you will see that this is it. And then, you say, where can you go? What more is there to attain when you have nothing to attain from the very start? And so you sit there. We see you. Where does he go, we wonder? What does he see that we don't? What is it like to be awake?

You, fraudulent striver, fraudulent practitioner of the way. Speaking of the path. The art of kensho rehearsal. Sitting there, rehearsing. You must not rehearse, you tell yourself, rehearsing that as well. You must not practice the art of concealment of self from self. You must not fill your life with must must must must must. You sit there. How can I present my insight? What can I say to show I have nothing to say? How deeply enlightened I already must be. But if I think this how can I be awake? Am I a fraud? Am I an impostor?

You sitting there. You sitting there seeing the living Buddha at the center of all centers, in this hall of finding yourself, losing yourself, sitting there when you should be sitting here. You should be here at all times, at all times here. Why can you not relax?

You ritualizing the art of forgetting ritual. You ritualizing non-rituals. You ritualizing the art of not ritualizing anything until there is nothing at all that has not become a ritual. You singing in the prophetic voice, there is nothing to proclaim, there is nothing to attain, I have seen it now! Steeped and soaked in fraudulence, terrified of your own insight, which you suspect may not be there.

You singing and singing and singing, locating that source of song somewhere deep in your abdomen, lower perhaps, even more within than your deepest within. You searching in the deepest anus of your belly for that which is your innermost, all the while thinking, this must be it, this cannot be it, I have no sense of me anymore, am I therefore enlightened?

You thinking to yourself, do I have a self or not? What is this? Is it true that I can wake up too? Am I already awake? Should I be bothered by this incessant wheezing to my side, this idiot meditator next to me who cannot control his fidgeting? Would it be more enlightened to put up with it or, with one word, one blow, to end his pain for him? What does the living Buddha think of me? What have I done to myself?

You the great fraudulent appeaser of your own desires. An infinite network of simultaneously growing and shrinking awarenesses all conspiring to undermine your progress. Who is aware? Is this the right direction?

The TRUE PRIEST is a fraud, he must be a fraud. The TRUE PRIEST knows nothing. I have never met a TRUE PRIEST worthy of the title. He sits here with the rest of us, letting us project our fantasies on to him, letting us perfect him ongoingly and unthinkingly. He sits here, he is here, but he lets us wonder whether he notices us drooling over him. He drools around like the rest of us when he is alone, imagines all sorts of idiotic things about himself, dreams them up and plays with them as he sits there pretending to be an enlightened man. He doesn't know shit. He sucked somebody's cock to get there. That's all it is. There aren't any TRUE PRIESTS, I've never met one. I do not say there is no Zen, only that there are no TRUE PRIESTS of Zen, that's what the koan was talking about. No such thing as enlightenment. No such thing as Buddhahood. It's all a crock of shit designed to keep us sitting here thinking we're different from the other religions. Who is "we" here? Who is different from the other religions? Who am I, I have to ask myself, ceaselessly. Who am I who am I who am I? At all times, the TRUE PRIEST tells me, I must sit here and ask myself who I am. Who am I, then? Don't try to engage with the question intellectually, the TRUE PRIEST told me. He said, he keeps on saying, focus on the asking. Don't try to answer, just focus on the asking. What the fuck does that mean? He doesn't know what he's talking about, and yet I find myself going along with it, like a donkey, like a child. Who am I? Who am I? Is that how he got here, this TRUE PRIEST? Constantly asking himself who he was, at all times, focusing on the asking itself instead of looking for an answer? And then boom, one day, a flash of insight that transformed every fiber of his being. Suddenly the man was a Buddha. And then he'll tell you, he always tells you, there is no such thing as enlightenment, you are already enlightened, you just have to see it for yourself. Should you attain awakening, you will see there is no difference between Nirvana and Samsara. Until then, you are trapped in dualistic thought. But don't worry about all that. Just focus on the question: who am I? At all times, in all places, whatever you're doing, focus on the question: who am I? Who am I? Yet this great TRUE PRIEST of mine, when I look at him, I don't see a Buddha. I see an ordinary human being, who insists he is perfectly ordinary, and lords over me at the same time telling me I too can reach enlightenment if I try my damnedest. And when I say he looks ordinary, I mean it: I am appalled by how ordinary he really is, he is a disgustingly human looking person. He farts, he burps, he laughs too loud, his breath reeks, he shits and wipes his ass. A monk asked Yun Men, "What is Buddha?" and Yun Men said, "A dried shit stick." Toilet paper. The Buddha is no more and no less than toilet paper. Stop your discriminating mind from discriminating mindlessly. Fret not, Rebecca. If you can see that the Buddha and whatever you use to wipe the shit from your asshole are indeed identical, you too can become a Buddha. If you can't, you remain shallowly floating about in a world of suffering, never knowing your own face. I swear to God my teacher is a fraud. All teachers, all prophets, everyone is just a fucking liar.

It doesn't matter what group I join, eventually it will prove to be a cult. The only thing stopping most groups from becoming cults is a lack of confidence in common sense, combined with an excess of confidence in a particular member of the group (no typo). This is so common that I can't even believe I'm sitting here with these people. One day, one of these assholes is going to have what he thinks is a major awakening, and our fraudulent priest will confirm his awakening, and then there is this suddenly confident, new, living Buddha. Then he's going to walk around telling everybody how enlightened he is, and this is going to turn everything around for people. There will be some who are jealous, who decide not only that this guy is a deluded asshole but also that the teacher has proven himself to be an impostor, and these will either leave or start up trouble within the group. There will be others who, unwilling to give up their investment in the group, in the sangha, confusedly look about in search of something to hold onto, wondering what they may have missed, wondering why this person suddenly is an enlightened bastard and everyone else is still wallowing in the dirt. This is how cults begin and end. Some people get promoted for no reason, others get demoted for no reason, some people get it and others don't get it at all, and then you get a whole bunch of increasingly insecure people wondering whether to follow or abandon their increasingly confident Masters. I can't believe I'm sitting here, meditating my way to awakening with these people, even though I'm keenly aware of the danger. What's wrong with me?

Bullshit bullshit bullshit. Who am I? Bullshit is all I am. I am one writhing mess of maggots, memories and melodrama. My mother and father were born after I will die. I was born before my original face killed the cat. I shouldn't be here. It's all bullshit, I want somebody to tell me I'm okay. That's all it is, someone to tell me I'm okay. Why do I need this so badly? Who am I who am I, at all times in all places continue to ask yourself: who am I?

It would be okay if the pain in my body weren't so bad, but it's terrible, and somehow it's getting worse the more I relax into it, I cannot manipulate myself into no longer manipulating myself. I have this ongoing feeling, or maybe it's a thought, but I have this kind of thought feeling perception at the back of my thoughts, this awareness that the more I try to manipulate myself and out-clever myself into giving up, the less I give up. I am not willing to let go. That's the problem here. I tell myself that making an effort is the wrong thing to do, that I need to let myself collapse once and for all, and just be here without trying. But I can't do it, can't just stop. So I have this constant worry that I'm trying too hard to be subtle about the way I manipulate my own thoughts to try and get somewhere without feeling like I'm trying to get somewhere. Oh my God. Oh my sweet forgotten Jesus Christ. The more I noticed myself doing this, the greater the pain in my legs, my knees, my back and shoulders and even my triceps, unbelievably. My fucking triceps hurt. They don't tell you about that one when they warn you that meditation is a physical thing. Even your triceps will hurt.

The false priest sees something in you, Rebecca. The false priest is full of wisdom, endlessly compassionate. But not really, not endlessly. Whoever could be endlessly compassionate? Is there such a thing? Do you aspire to an impossible ideal, or is nothing impossible for those for whom emptiness is lived? The TRUE PRIEST, the master, has guided you well. It's hard to remember exactly why there was so much rage the other day; The other session, this morning. It's difficult to remember now, difficult to remember, difficult. So much rage, so much resentment. Where did it all come from? What happened? What is this?

"It's always the fucking same," Rebecca told McGeeee. It was the most profoundly dishonest thing she'd ever said to him — perhaps not the most significant lie, but the lie emptiest of truth — and she hoped never to find herself forced to take it back. An evasion: that was all. It's always the fucking same — with her mother, with herself, their relationship. Before then, she had always presented a mostly accurate, mostly boring picture of Rebecca and Her Mother. The mother and daughter who could not quite get along, who loved each other only by implication, who tried and failed and tried and failed again. And would continue like this, at least in McGeeee's mind. He must be made to believe in the continuity of that failure. She had to persuade him that nothing had changed, that they had failed once again to bond, when, for the first time, they had been honest with each other and triumphed. It was horrible, unbelievable, but a triumph in the end, the ultimate clicking-together. And none of McGeeee's business. Nobody's. The revelation, Mildred's confession, had been meant for nobody else, and though Rebecca suspected and hoped she would never speak to her mother again, she intended to honor the confidence, not merely out of shame but respect for the gift. So McGeeee must never know.

He never would. She refused to tell him what had happened, even in lies. Only variations of: "It's always the fucking same," aiming to hint that the cycle of endless failure had in fact ended because they had failed too many damned times. She'd had enough. It was over, she had no mother anymore, leave her alone. And he did. He prodded occasionally, then his curiosity seemed to fade, and they lived a pseudo-marriage. Or a real marriage. Even that wasn't clear to her now: whether her mother's confession had somehow been a rite of initiation, too, the inauguration of Rebecca's new life as complicit in the art of falsehood and incompleteness. Mildred had spent her adult life avoiding or actively fighting away the power of truth to become common property. She held on to truth with jealousy, and maybe the hope that her tenacity made her, at least in one sense, heroic. She had constructed a world for everyone to share and she had excluded herself from it: to the world, Mildred was a woman with secrets like anyone else, a woman to be respected like anyone else, while in her own mind she remained something else entirely. She was a secret with human qualities, shielding herself from discovery, resisting and gradually taming the impulse to speak herself out loud so that others might judge her.

PRAISE OF MOTHERHOOD, PART ONE

The coffin looked heavy but held nothing more than a corpse, which is nothing. A careless funeral, fast, bury her as soon as you can, move on, there are things to do. And the woman in the coffin had died quickly, too, and her daughter didn't want to speak, her son-in-law had only met the woman once, the false priest knew he was not welcome, and the others, the few that came, stayed quiet because there is very little to say when you never loved the deceased. The son-in-law looked at his wife who looked at her mother in the coffin staring into absolute blackness, hearing nothing. There in the coffin the woman was dead for good, and her daughter seemed unmoved, and her son-in-law thought *what's the point attending your mother's funeral if you know you never loved her* and rested his hands in his pockets as his own mother had taught him not to do, the son-in-law whose hobby was honoring the dead he had never known strolling through the graveyards as a boy and as a man still, reading the epitaphs engraved on forgotten rocks covered with moss and always damp even in summer. The woman in the coffin had seemed kind enough but her daughter had despised her with the very blood she shared with her, a loathing so intense her simple presence here today was a remarkable thing noted by the others, whom he did not know and would not know once the funeral was over. The false priest spoke meek and shy into the ground and glanced from time to time at the faces of the men and women around him, wondering.

The son-in-law, McGeeee, considered but ended up not placing his hand on his wife's shoulder because he knew, or suspected with a sad unbitter resignation, that she'd shake the hand off and go back to standing very still and very silent inviting no touch. She didn't want it, and would resent him for what she would end up calling condescension at the best and worst moment of her life. Or perhaps he was reading her badly, perhaps she felt a bottomless and terrible sympathy for her mother at last and she needed the comforting. But to risk irritating her at her mother's funeral, he would not and probably couldn't dare because in the end he was a simple coward. He was a coward and couldn't for the sake even of simple self-respect place his hand on the shoulder of a woman he loved to reassure her, for fear of upsetting her, though he, too, was upset, from the sheer callousness he saw in his wife's posture and the indifference with which everyone treated the dead's departure.

And he thought *somewhere around here someone must have loved this woman or at least someone can tell me why nobody loved her* but he was in the front row and could not raise his head too drastically or they would notice and consider him cold. He thought *I am bored and shouldn't be, but I am bored at a funeral, my wife's mother's funeral* and he understood briefly before forgetting again that this really had nothing to do with him, he might or might not have attended and nobody would have cared, not even his wife, who in her almost insane rigidity would never even look his way until the ordeal was done with and she could finally tell the truth when she told people her mother was dead. This had nothing to do with him. He stood unmoving.

There were no children and in fact no one younger than his wife. The clearing of throats and coughing, smokers and people far older than him. The smokers. He thought of the lungs in that little corpse, rotten and atrophied, the woman who smoked two packs a day, before and during and after meals, who had shaken his hand too quickly because she needed to tip the ashes. He could remember only the intimidating glances she cast and the urine smell of cigarettes. And his wife, back then a fiancée, still eager to please him and make sure he was comfortable in his seat and didn't go to bed hungry, had made conversation a little too eagerly, boisterously, forcing a bond between her mother and her man that would never spring of its own accord. And then they had argued, the mother and the daughter, whatever about, always the same, according to his fiancée the problem was always the fucking stupid same, but she never said what the problem was. Then the phone call the next day. She'd locked herself in the bedroom with the phone and reemerged an hour later in tears, saying, "This time I mean it. I will never speak to her again."

"But what happened?" he'd said, and she, taking his face in her hands and kissing his nose and sniffling herself to some state of decorum, said, "Nothing. The problem is that nothing happened. I don't want to talk about it."

"Did she hate me? Does she not approve?"

"It has nothing to do with you. And let's not talk about it."

And for the few years they'd known each other they said nothing about it. No calls from the mother-in-law, no mention of her, no pictures. The woman had never existed anymore. So that when the news had come from her Aunt Martha — "She did not want you to know. She wanted to keep you out of the loop completely. I'm so sorry. I should have told you as soon as she was diagnosed. God, I feel like an idiot..." — it was as if a stranger's death had been announced, a woman they'd maybe heard of but knew nothing about, which in his case was almost true, though he had wondered why they had stopped speaking, and what role he might have played in the rupture. And now the funeral, a ceremony his wife had decided to attend, as if to have the last laugh. But he could not imagine her so cruel. It was to say goodbye. She had loved her mother after all. And soon she would break down, and he would be there to comfort her. All those bottled up feelings. It wasn't healthy. She would need to talk. If she wanted him, he was there. If she didn't, he would stay out of her way. That woman's ghost would linger above them for a while, but it, too, would die eventually. Then the marriage could begin properly, licit and acceptable, assuming, as he always did without knowing why, that the rupture really had been because of him. Because he might have cast an impression so unfavorable, even so repulsive, that the rotting bridge between mother and daughter finally crumbled. That was only a possibility, but it haunted him. Yet in his soberer moments he knew it really had nothing to do with him. It was a secret war between them to which he had never contributed.

He stood there, looking at his wife, scratching his thigh through his pocket, trying without really trying to listen to the priest's words. But perhaps he fell asleep or time tricked him; the oration was soon over, a short unfelt procedure, followed by a silence and a general hesitation and, finally, someone shrugged and announced that the coffin would be lowered into the ground. And it was. They were far enough from the city not to hear the sounds of traffic. He noticed that. Then he watched the dirt spreading over the coffin and considered the birdsong all around. His wife stared on ahead, refusing perhaps to look straight at the box holding the object of her hate. Nobody cried. McGeeee, captivated by the birds chirping their meaningless message over the event, felt his wife's hand clasp his. She had looked, seen the death. The cold damp hand slippery in his, digging fingers into his palm. Now he didn't dare look at her, or she might begin to cry.

When the funeral and the various silences were all over, when enough people had said that there was really nothing to say — never, he noticed, stooping to paying the dead woman a compliment, for nobody had loved her; that was clear, and very sad, but perhaps he did not know enough — when the priest had lowered his head enough times although he had not known the woman and could have told you nothing about her, and when everyone was gone, the son-in-law stood at the grave with his wife in a perfect serenity. Neither spoke for a few minutes. Her eyes were fixed on her mother's name. The tombstone was made of marble. A cross above the other engravings. A cross — the cross of Christ, whose name had filled his wife with revulsion, she who mocked the religious and the irreligious equally for the faith they placed in ghosts, who knew the lines of the crucifix, spreading to infinity as they might, would always converge at that irrational spot. She had shared her thoughts early on, her bitter views on the sad need in people for a semblance of balance. "They use religion for their sense of the world and if they don't have religion they use science, but they're deluding themselves either way." And he had listened because she seemed to care. Genius or imbecile, man or woman, everyone looked for a center and shied away from the boundless. And Christ was that figure standing between the now and the infinite, at a safe distance from either extremity, tiny man and enormous God combined in a great paradox. She had rambled and ranted, never making all the sense she might have tried to make, but passionate, quietly and coolly determined to show him she had opinions. That had been before he'd met her mother. And now the mother was lying beneath their feet, and he looked at his wife without knowing what to say, wanting, maybe, to ask very subtly why she had given her mother a Christian funeral when neither mother nor daughter had ever wanted the slightest thing to do with religion.

Then she spoke, running a finger across the surface of the marble and looking at nothing: "I can't decide how much I really despised her."

"You never told me anything," he said. "I know so little about your relationship with her."

"There was no relationship. She raised me and didn't let me starve and I suppose I'm grateful for that. But standing here looking at this rock all I can think is: how much do I really care? Do I even have the energy to hate her? I'm like a giant to her now. She's nothing. And I can't tell if I'm sad or relieved or indifferent or anything at all."

"But you loved her. You're her daughter."

"How can I know what I feel? I didn't speak to her for two years. I've been married to you for a fraction of the time she spent taking care of me, but I still feel I know you better than I ever could know her. She stayed at home and never hired a nanny and fed and bathed and clothed me and I still don't think I know anything about her. She was so strange towards the end." And to the tombstone: "I want to call you a bitch, but I don't know why. So goodbye instead."

They remained there another minute, before she took his hand and said, "Let's go to the car. I don't think I'm even sad anymore."

They drove back toward the city, listening to no music and saying nothing at all. He glanced at her: the way she rested her hands on the wheel as if she wanted to stroke it, the slight stiffness of her movements, the constant sighs. She drove as she'd always driven, patiently, slowly, getting frustrated at nobody in particular, enjoying very little of it. It was only when they were close to home, after they'd beaten the lunchtime traffic and each had privately realized that they had the rest of the day ahead of them and no plans and a lot of things to talk about, that she slowed the car down, parked with a clumsiness she didn't usually permit herself and said, "I feel awful about one thing. No, two things. I feel awful about not feeling awful about my mother's death. And I feel awful because I gave her a religious funeral even though I knew she would have hated that."

"Why did you do it?"

"I think I'm cruel."

"You're not cruel. Or maybe you are. But there's got to be more to it."

"She hated everything about religion. I hate it too. But I didn't want that in common with her, maybe. I don't know. It's such a petty thing. And now it feels like the biggest offense. Her brother was a priest."

"I didn't even know she had a brother."

"I never met him. He was the middle child. He died years ago. They fell out about his faith. Can you imagine? I'm just like her, really — I cut ties with people because of what they fail to be. My uncle wasn't enough of a free-thinker for her and she wasn't enough of a decent human being for me. She fell out with her mother too. All of them dead now. And I'm following in her footsteps, maybe. I broke off contact with her and then she died and one day, if people remember, they'll say the same thing about me that I say about my mother: *she cut ties with those who loved her; the bitch couldn't accept them for who they were.*"

"You're exaggerating."

"I'm not. I feel like I did everything wrong. I handled it all badly. There was no need to stop talking to her."

"Are you finally going to tell me why you fell out?"

"Not now. Maybe. Maybe later."

They spent the afternoon doing very little. He made her coffees. She vacuumed, and refused to let him help. "I need a distraction." He'd expected her to speak about her mother. She spoke instead of the future. "Do you think I should quit working? For a while, anyway?"

"Why would you do that?"

"Because I'm feeling inspired to do it. We both know we'd survive if only you worked for a few months. I know it's not fair. If my mother had left me something, I'd make the decision right now. But I want to talk to you about it."

"But why?"

"I don't know. I think I need time to figure things out. I would like to travel."

"I can't travel with you if I'm still working."

"I know."

They stared at each other. She was still dressed in black, and she looked older, more assured, than he'd ever seen her. He stood and turned the kettle on again. "That would mean not seeing you for a while."

She seemed to force a smile. "I think I need to escape. Maybe I'm just being a little girl. I don't know. Yeah, maybe I'm not being reasonable."

"Where would you go?"

"No idea."

"Aren't you happy? Apart from today and all that today means, aren't you happy living here, with me?"

"You can't take it personally, McGeeee. Please don't take this personally. I'm sorry. I am happy."

"Then why do you want to go away?"

"I'm not going *away*, I just want to travel. I'm not leaving *you*. I'd be back."

"Then let's go together."

"How is that realistic? You've got a career building up. I'm freelance. Think about this. I'm sorry — you have a right to be mad. But I'm not saying anything about our marriage."

"I'm not mad. Let me think about this. Give me a moment."

The moment dragged on. He went for a walk. The pavement was covered in dead leaves, red and yellow and brittle, crackling under his feet. They are more beautiful when they die. A shriveled crackling leaf is beautiful because it has died. And he thought of the dead woman set into the ground, buried under dirt and history. When we die we repulse the others, even and especially those who loved us, those who touched us. When leaves die we rake them up and burn them like bodies but we sigh with wonderment because they illuminate the streets. He wasn't fooling himself. He was not interested in leaves. Thoughts of her, and her wanting to leave for a while. For traveling and possibly never coming back. Because she might be bored with him. Now she had lost her mother and it was a perfect, convenient, just cruel opportunity, leave him in the wake of a death he knew he had to respect but could not much care about. She could say she was leaving because the death had shaken her up, when in fact she just needed an excuse to leave. She was going to leave him. This, in the end, if he trusted his instincts, was about him and her and not the dead woman.

He walked past a sitting homeless man who did not ask for change. A bearded but neat-looking youngish redheaded man, so skinny he perhaps lacked even the energy to beg. And reaching into his pocket the son-in-law slowed, turned back and said, "You need a bit of change?" thinking if I do this maybe I can forget about what is actually important, which is not this man's life but my life with the woman I love but can't keep. "You want a bit of money?"

"No, thank you," and the homeless unbegging man stared on into the space in front of him.

"So that's that," and he carried on walking, thinking if I could just make someone's day better karma will favor me today, knowing it wouldn't because karma is another sack of shit, but hoping as we do and thinking maybe what she wants is to commit suicide although that was unlikely because she was not that kind of woman. But for just that reason she might do it. Whatever had happened with her mother in the past, whatever guilt she could be carrying around — would that be enough for her to do it? And how would she do it? He was back in the dead leaves, walking home again. He scratched his neck, I need to cut these nails, and found it odd, even unsettling, that only a few hours before he had been standing at the grave of a woman who'd lived many more years than he had and now simply didn't exist except as deterioration. His father, still alive and still old, but for how long, had told him once never to forget that death is not as scary as children and grownups think, that death is only scary if you don't understand how horrible life would be without it. And that was the whole talk on death. His mother then took him aside and explained that Daddy was very sad because Daddy's own daddy, your grandfather, had just died, and if Daddy seemed strange for the next few days it was not your fault and you shouldn't worry about upsetting Daddy but at the same time you should try to behave and be good and not get in anyone's way until Daddy felt better. And the son had understood little but just enough to stay out of trouble, another way of dying sometimes. Now the son was a grownup and Daddy was no longer sad because of his father but sad because of Mommy who wasn't there anymore; and the son's own wife had lost her mother and was very sad for that reason too; everyone dealing with everyone else's death. Somewhere the ghosts were gathering.

McGeeee could see his home, the walls around his wife, sitting in there, maybe crying or maybe slicing some ham for a sandwich or listening to the radio she'd brought with her from her mother's house along with one dress ("It was always meant to be my dress, I think...") and some photographs of a family dog, if there had been a dog. Was she thinking of him at all, of what she'd say to appease him, or convince him that leaving was for the best, that she'd return soon but needed to be alone (with a lover or with sister-friends she had never mentioned) just long enough to sort her problems out ("without encumbering you"), to clear her head ("I feel suffocated in all this freedom"), to find out what she really wanted to do now that her mother and everything that her mother had stood for ("the bitch inside me, not a real bitch but the hidden fragment of evil within that I had to bottle up so I would never become my mother") had disappeared for ever?

But his wife was gone when he walked in. He called her name and checked inside the bedroom, and the study, and he knocked on the bathroom door then opened it and there was nobody inside. The living room was empty. Her cell phone was lying on the table. She couldn't be far. She'd gone to buy milk, or bread, or she was speaking to the neighbors. Or she had decided to leave him at once. Perhaps she had never existed. He sat on the leather couch in the living room and rubbed the leather with his knuckles. He hated the couch. If she had left him, the couch would go too. And he thought: along the way somewhere she has decided I'm too much of a coward for her to love me, and she's right. But this wasn't about him.

When she returned with a bag of groceries in her hand she found him crying on the leather couch. She stared a few seconds then placed the bag on the table and sat by his side.

"McGeeee." He kept crying. "McGeeee. Come on. It's okay."

"It's okay," he said. "I know it's okay." He didn't look up.

"Why are you crying?"

"I don't know. I feel stupidly emotional. I don't know why I'm crying."

"What happened on your walk?"

"Why were you gone? That's what I started crying about. I have no idea why it bothered me so much."

"I went to buy stuff at the store," she said. She held his hand. "What happened?"

"Nothing. I don't know."

They sat and he felt his face dry up slowly. She kissed him. "Thank you for being sweet."

"When was I sweet?"

"I just mean, I shouldn't even have brought it up. The whole going away thing. I don't need to go anywhere. I think we're both a bit stressed out, and you've been putting up with me and I appreciate that. And you tend to bottle things up inside. Maybe you simply needed to cry."

"I feel weak," he said. "I'm going to nap."

He undressed right there and bundled up his pants and shirt and took them with him to the bedroom, tossed them against the wall, and slipped into the bed. A few minutes later he was asleep.

When he woke, his wife was gone.

She'd left her phone on the kitchen table, and a short, almost trivial note: *I have to go, McGeeee. I won't be back.* That was it. Sort of impersonal, barely legible. Not even the courtesy of an explanation, a lie, a hint. *I have to go, McGeeee.* I. Have. To. Go. She *had* to go. *She* had to go. And she wouldn't be back. That was it. And perhaps that was all he needed to know. The explanation was there. Everything else, the justifications, the infuriating implications, all that was stupid, an unacceptable indulgence; the two things he needed to know, he knew, and that was it. But he had stared at the note, scratched his chin, not quite shocked, nothing, letting nothing sink in just yet, examining the scrawls, thinking: I have overslept. And laughing, a little more nervous, and thinking: I slept her out of existence. The prickling of a tear in his eye but nothing else. The downpour could wait. And all he could say aloud, to nobody: "Oh damn it." Somehow not surprised, not even angry. Barely able to think, then thinking nothing at all, looking straight at the curves of her handwriting until they seemed like worms caught under a blade, meaningless, idiotic, pointless, absurd and very upsetting. Thinking nothing but staring and letting the meaninglessness spread from his mind to his muscles and from there to the world that wasn't him, atoms and light and heat all doing their work without a purpose and that is the condition you find yourself in so why must it matter so much if you can't have her quite the same way that you had her once upon a time oh my God that fucking cunt that absolute bitch leaving thinking she can fuck off while I'm asleep and I can do no fucking thing about it

because she is gone

God fucking damn it

God fucking cunt

fucking bitch fuck

PRAISE OF MOTHERHOOD, PART TWO

A large brown envelope in the mailbox. It was for Rebecca.

McGeeee thought he recognized the handwriting next to the stamps. Uneven, graceless, feminine-unfeminine, busy doctor's handwriting. The envelope was full almost to the point of bursting. He took it inside, and placed it on the table, along with the prescription pills he'd picked up at the pharmacy. This sudden reminder of how everything had changed, and how new limits had been set between him and his wife, made him shudder. He knew, and was even almost happy to admit aloud, that by now he should have tried to contact someone who knew where Rebecca might be. Maybe Rita, or Rebecca's relatives, or mutual friends. He would receive no sympathy from anyone anymore: he'd simply let her leave and had done nothing about it. It would appear to others that he didn't care, that his selfishness had reached new heights. And that might even be true at this point. He didn't need her. He'd grown used to missing her, to pinning his hopes on her always-delayed return. Now that she'd left, he could spend the rest of his days convincing himself all of his problems had begun the day she'd left. Before that, life was a paradise. After, it was endless torment, and there was a romantic side to that. It was all about fooling yourself.

But the envelope on the table, when he returned from the kitchen with a glass of water, would change everything. Even as he opened it, giving no thought to Rebecca's privacy — that non-issue from a past life — he could sense that something was about to happen. Because the letter was addressed to Rebecca, instead of being from her to him, he'd cared little at first. If she'd never left, he'd simply have handed it to her and then casually asked what had been in it a few hours later. But now he was about to get a glimpse into her secret world. This wasn't just an envelope stuffed with bills or legal information; he knew the handwriting on it, even if he couldn't place it, and this was the first proof of Rebecca's having even existed since she'd left.

Inside the envelope was a smaller, white envelope, as well as many dozens of postcards, a small blue notebook, letters and photographs. Before opening the white envelope he shuffled through the pictures. They were old, once in black and white, faded and aged now to the point of yellowness. Pictures of a young girl surrounded by little boys. The girl wore dresses; the boys were younger than her, and all of them wore sailor outfits, without exception, from picture to picture. On the back of the largest picture, a family portrait that seemed to include the mother of the children as well as a very old man dressed in pajamas and a middle-aged woman so fat she took up a significant part of the image, someone had written some names. He couldn't make out any except Peter, and perhaps Mildred — the name of Rebecca's mother and, he presumed, the name of the little girl standing by the very fat woman's side. He stared at the face for a long while: the monkey grin, the curls in Mildred's hair, the weird and ambivalent knowledge that she was dead now.

Before turning to the postcards and letters, McGeeee opened the small white envelope. It was addressed to nobody. Inside it, a single white card with the following scrawled on it:

My dear Rebecca, I don't know if I'm doing the right or the wrong thing in sending you this, but I think you will understand when you've gone through it, if you go through it. Here are some of the letters from your mother that your grandmother and your uncle McDurrrr received from your mother when she was young, as well as some pictures from your mother's childhood. Both McDurrrr and your Granny Grumps kept the letters even after your mother cut ties with them — a horrible moment for everyone. You'll also find a single letter written by McDurrrr, which we found in your mother's drawers with various other things, and some postcards that were in there too — and that weird little blue notebook which McDurrrr kept when he was younger and which might shed some insight into his "artistic" side. Finally, I'm including letters that your mother wrote to your cousin Gerald. Before he died, Gerald asked me to give everything that had ever been his away, and to be honest, I don't know who else I should give these letters to. So I hope you'll forgive me for sending you this; I didn't want to throw it away. You will see, in these letters, how much your mother loved you and how proud she was up until the end, even after you disappeared from her life. I'm sorry I sound accusatory; I don't mean to sound like I disapprove. Your mother was difficult and so were you back then. I hope that through these little artifacts you'll be able to understand your mother's point of view a little better. Give McGeeee my regards, and I hope we see each other sooner than the next time there's a funeral.

Love,

your Aunt Martha.

Now here's a world…

A whole complicated, impenetrable world Rebecca had never shared with him. He put the letter down and looked at the postcards. Most of them came from Europe: this one from Paris; that one had a picture of the Belem Tower in Lisbon, but the stamp was Spanish:

Dearest Millie,

Portugal was strange. What an atmosphere. Things are not so stable there, and it was a mistake, at least a political one, to go. Well, political — who cares about that. We are in Spain now. It's a nicer country. Anywhere is better than America right now, though, and we'd never go back if you and your siblings weren't waiting for us to return! I love you — Your Mother (missing you!!!) And this one, from Prague: *Millie-Millie-Millie: Just a quick reminder that your mother loves you. Greetings from Prague!*

He put the postcards down and, sipping his water, tried to understand. He'd seen Mildred's body lowered into the earth; he'd stood at her grave with her conflicted daughter. The letter in the white envelope, in that handwriting he'd recognized, had come from Martha, Rebecca's aunt, Mildred's sister. She'd sent packages and flowers to the house before; she had always been kind to McGeeee, and somehow appeared to know theirs was not to be a lasting marriage. She'd treated McGeeee as you'd treat a friend's child, familiarly but with a little hesitation, a slice of fear. And Martha, as he thought he remembered, had been adopted. She was the eldest — if the brother, the priest, was, as Rebecca had called him, the middle-child, then Mildred was the youngest. And whoever their mother was — that single reference to Granny Grumps made little sense to him, since the postcards Mildred had received from her mother implied anything but a grumpy old matriarch — she had, it seemed, been an adventurous spirit, traveling to Spain, to Portugal, to Prague, at a time when these were not the safest or most welcoming of places, nor, presumably, the easiest countries to visit as a tourist.

The next letter he read had been written on brittle lined paper, and the pages were stapled together at the top-right corner. The handwriting, this time, was agitated, almost rebellious, a series of hieroglyphically unreadable lines and scratched-out scribbles and jots and dashes. At first he could barely make out any words, and wasn't even sure it was written in English. It took him a couple of minutes to begin to understand what he was reading:

Millie,

I can't & wouldn't anyway if I could come to terms with the sheer pure stupidity of your words & I hope that someone somewhere manages to break you down to the point of humility & tearfulness. You have hurt me more than you probably know or care. From the time we were children running around playing with the toys appropriate to our ages you always had to condescend to me, to mock

& belittle me for the sake of some twisted fantasy of entitlement you needed above all else to maintain. Yours is a fragile (& ever ready, ever eager to collapse) universe of self-importance. You need to be destroyed. I know, also, what you will say to this letter, if you bother to reply at all (I ask you not to reply if all I can expect is the sort of unbecoming but strangely consistent venom you've shown me all your life). You will laugh it off as yet more proof of my emotional immaturity, of my need to live in the grace of a God I will never come to terms with (& somehow of course this is reason enough to ridicule me, even though I AM TRYING at least to make some sense of this universe & my place inside it). You will tell yourself you were right to say all those hurtful things to my face for no other reason than that you could. Millie, in the end you are nothing more than the monster our mother always feared you'd be & I am sorry, disappointed, shamed & terrified to put it like that while knowing as fully as I do that it's true, that all of this is the child of your own cruelty & our appeasement of your whims.

I was so revolted by your precious opinions (of which you have far too many to be consistent) that I wasn't able to defend myself when we saw each other. So let me tell you, if you are still reading, if you haven't already forgotten that you were reading this letter, that I never deserved to be called a coward, intellectual or emotional. I am not a coward, Millie. It is not out of a quality of cowardice that I let myself embrace the presence of something else. To you, the frock is no better than the gun that makes the gangster. You say I'm crippled by my insecurities & somehow you say it without even blinking, without caring that your older brother, who helped you when the neighborhood kids used to tease you, who held your hand at your father's funeral, without caring that this older brother has been struggling with what perhaps can be called despair, or hopelessness, or a million other words that only hint at the empty & gaping monstrosity Mankind has felt from the moment there was such a thing as Time — you don't care & of course you don't, why should you, you whose only concern is MILLIE & MILLIE

& MILLIE FOREVER, & damn everything that doesn't conform to Millie's vision of the world. Since your vision would not sit comfortably next to mine, & since there can in your eyes only be a SINGLE vision, you feel the need to crush my perspective out of existence. Remorseless, uncaring, unaware, incapable of accepting that yours is not the role of the Savior, & I don't mean Christ, whose love you reject anyway & so be it for now, I mean any kind of Savior — you think as soon as you grew into a woman (& to be honest, Millie, you are not yet 22 years old, you are hardly a woman in any but the most pedantic legal sense) & as soon as your opinions were found oh so interesting by a few of the boys you dated in school & a couple of imperceptive teachers whose asses you kissed with your brilliance, you were somehow appointed — what, Savior of Mankind? Too clever to be kind? Too wise to be considerate & so you can roam the world pointing out what you think is everyone's fatal flaw? Because you are exempt? Because you alone are capable of bliss & completion?

I am not a coward, not a fool, not a charlatan. Your judgments mean nothing to you, they come easy as breathing, & having pronounced them you feel better & expect those around you to forgive & thank you for your cruelty. I do not forgive you, Millie. Nor do I thank you. I am indeed a flawed man, as you are a flawed young woman & everything I do is meant to make the people I love happier, more RIGHT & UNAFRAID in this place. Yours is the opposite mentality. You will surely think, in the comfort of your arrogance, that because I tell you that I cannot forgive you, I must be a hypocritical man of God. You will think that because your cruelty has moved me to write this letter out of a desperate need for vindication & revenge, I must fall into that unsurprisingly enormous category of human beings who claim to dedicate their lives to worshipping the Father while failing to meet their own standards & the standards he set for them every single day. Perhaps & not just perhaps that is the fundamental problem, of course — your incapacity to understand that the very point of my faith, the point of all faiths worth speaking about, is that MAN IS FLAWED & cannot measure up to the infinite potential he believes lies within himself, inaccessible but there & someday to be his. To you all of this is fakery & superstition. You think you can dismiss my profession & my life's mission by shooting the sleeping sparrow you call religion — meanwhile the hawk of God continues to circle overhead. Perhaps the cowardice here is yours. If you were only able to accept that a love of God is not the same as an uncritical approval of everything that organized religion (even my own) has done in the name of that love & its divine reciprocation, then we might have a chance at loving each other as siblings & as human beings. But until you get over your undeserved sense of ultimate superiority — I will do exactly as you asked, & let you consider me a lost brother, or perhaps a revealed enemy. You will not hear from me again for any petty reason. You asked that I stay out of your life & so I will. Perhaps we will meet at another funeral.

Yours,

McDurrrr

PS. A very few people will ever know what you do, what you have let me know in part. They will go their lives crawling through the dark thinking what have I done & how can I make it right. They will do anything & more to get their greedy claws (& we are all greedy & we all come equipped with claws, I must not seem to be passing judgment) on something like peace, never knowing never doubting never even able to consider the idea that you, your way, your violent decree, you are the way to peace. You & your love for nothing, you & your love of the great big nothing-void-abyss, you are the only thing that can empty us of our urges & desires or at least their pressure. When they come to you too late in their beds waiting to join what they think will be their partner in death & their breath clouds up their glasses through which they cannot even see anyway & their finger-claws are no longer capable of gripping anything at all: that is when it is no longer any use to find you. You are you,

you are to be addressed, not confessed to. You are a way of speaking & listening. You are a method of understanding & explaining. Can they see this? Can they possibly grasp the method of you, the life technique that you are? Only some & of course they feel abandoned so often. They come to you so late in their lives. They seek to redress the balance when the fear of death grips them tightest. By then you gain proportions in their imaginations so great you become a source of terror. You are not terror. You are a mechanism & a kettle & an army knife, not the oil in the machine, not the water in the kettle, not the block of wood we whittle away at with the uncompromising idleness of children. You are not substance or essence, you are tactic and system. You are not the mystery of the soul, you are the rules in the game. You are strategy & structure. You are evidence & procedure. When the secret of life evades us, we look for it elsewhere; but you are not the secret; you are the words we use to speak of the possibility of secrets. When they preach your love, the wisest among them are in fact preaching your process. I believe in no heaven, no hell. I believe in the activity of belief.

I have stopped to consider our method, our communication. You speak only through motion so I am always & sometimes frustratedly alert to the activity of your mind in the most trivial things. My routines & my daily banalities: are they helping me to see your patterns, or must I break them apart to see how everything works? If my life were a cupboard or better yet the concept of a cupboard & the drawers my years & the wood my body — where would you lurk? What they call paranoia they can attach to me as a stupid arrogant label anytime they want. Why don't they? Because I have joined those who believe themselves entitled to speak on your behalf & why not? When my sister, whose life, I think & fear, will amount to a continual renunciation of system, decides to speak to me again, if she decides it, what can I tell her? Will my faith in your process have dwindled? Am I insane? Millie is a million different voices all screaming into one telephone. How can I make sense of her? What is there to learn of you in the noise? She cannot accept & will never be able to accept that just because she is a mere cog in your machine (as are we all) does not mean she cannot be special — since the whole shines through her particularity, the universal resides in her uniqueness.

McGeeee couldn't go on reading this insanity, couldn't focus. Such commitment. He put the letter down and left the living room. He paced: from the bedroom to the basement, around the basement, picking up items he knew he'd end up throwing away, moving boxes of old clothes with his feet. Rebecca's clothes. He would burn them someday. Even if only to keep warm. He'd smell traces of her skin in the flames. He went to bed. He slept.

CONDEMNATION OF MOTHERHOOD

Rebecca had once walked with someone, a *man*, with opinions and experience, patience, impatience. How old was she then? Perhaps not yet seventeen. Old enough, at least, to know what he wanted, and young enough to believe herself capable of giving it.

"Because what was it that Enrique Des Pasito said about the life of the..."

No, older than seventeen. Because she'd started on that path — the academic life, which ended up not holding much life at all — just after turning eighteen. She'd headed off to her little campus about a week after turning into a near-adult. There she'd met him, a lecturer, but not her lecturer. Only a man from that world, with research credentials in something nobody he taught cared about. And it was frustrating, he said. Because the university is a haven for complacency, arrogance and the permission to be angry. He wasn't angry, he said, insisted. He was only, what, disappointed.

"Maybe not even disappointed, I'm only, well, I see the world a little more clearly now that I realize I'm too much in it."

She hadn't listened, much, even then. What mattered was his complicity in the anger. He was from there, that haven of complacency, and his disappointment was little more, in the end, than passionless rage at the unfairness of the world. She walked with him, nodded, probed, asked naive questions, and thought about anger. Its role in her own life: anger at her mother, anger at whatever. But at least she had passion. When the walk was over, the lecturer, exhausted by his own rant, had offered his number. He held out a card with a trembling, sweat-shiny hand. She had taken it. After two weeks of brief and increasingly furtive encounters, he invited her to his apartment. She declined, then changed her mind, then declined again. He felt led on. He said so. It seemed like an adolescent complaint. She never saw him again: on a campus able to hold only a couple thousand people, including staff, she never bumped into the lecturer again.

Most of her days she spent reading and ignoring those who wanted *something* from her. After classes she went for coffee with a friend, until the friend became her lover and she decided to end that too. Then she made a new friend. She'd made at least six friends by graduation, who never met each other. She could only handle people one-on-one. This made her seem more mysterious than she was.

Over time the memory of that lecturer, with his rage at the university, at the world and at himself, turned out to inspire her. She wrote him a letter, which became a novel. She spent a few weeks writing it, showing it to nobody, and then, when she suddenly and brutally realized it was going nowhere, she gave up on it. She didn't try her hand at writing fiction again until she married McGeeee. By then she had lost all her college friends. She'd made more on the way: a trip to Europe left her briefly infatuated with a young man from Paris, to whom the sexual act was terrifying and grotesquely exaggerated in its beauty. A two-week stay in Romania made her feel somehow more connected than she had ever been to people, to her body, to her mind: by the time she'd married McGeeee, she wasn't able to explain, even to herself, why a tiny romance with a Romanian bartender had managed to transform her so completely. But she never thought about him now. Somehow the perfection of their fling had turned the memory of him into an almost disgusting embarrassment. It had been too good. She forbade herself her nostalgia.

Time passed occasionally. She went through stretches of boredom and reading, then time jolted her into the near future where everything had been moving on except her: eventually she had to buy a cell phone, because otherwise how will we communicate with you, and soon she was on the internet reading articles about books and philosophers. She dated a musician who considered himself a philosopher, and knew something about it. She absorbed and scribbled. He played her a song he'd recorded and she almost liked it, though she didn't understand music, its construction or its appeal. This upset him but he tried not to show it. When she asked him why her opinion mattered, he turned sad. "I just want to impress you. With what I love best. With what I love to do."

"You can impress me with your philosophy."

"I don't have one."

"I mean you can talk to me about it. About philosophy."

And he did. He'd done his reading, his thinking. He almost held opinions, but wasn't attached to any of them. This attracted her. It gave her, uh, the phrase is — ontological substance. The depth of his knowledge made her feel real. She quickly discovered she didn't care a bit for Kant's categorical imperative, because it tried, metaphysically, to account for freedom as the, what, the autonomy of the will, was it? The way he'd explained it, she didn't give a damn. But she cared about his explanation. She listened as they moved on to Hegel, who wanted to surpass and correct Kant through, again, what was it, the point was that understanding causal relations wasn't enough, there was more to be grasped, something conceptual that could bring us back to the way things worked without relying on — he'd said science, "but not science as Hegel uses the word, I mean science today, which is stuck at the level of..." and he'd used a phrase she couldn't quite remember, but they focused on the first two parts of the *Phenomenology*, skipping the boring bits until he realized they *couldn't* skip the boring bits because "you see, right there, in the Preface, where he says...well, I can't find where he says it, but the point is that you need to follow the arguments in their total complexity to see why, for instance, consciousness reaches its deadlock at the particular moments that it does, and why we then need to take the nature of consciousness itself as a *relation* into account."

"He kind of implies it right here in the first paragraph," she said, and pointed at her own copy. *"For whatever it might be suitable to state about philosophy in a preface…this cannot be accepted as the form and manner in which to expound philosophical proof."*

"Yes, that's right, you can't just summarize, you see, it's… it's more than just a summary, Hegel's whole thing, project, uh, he's trying to lead us from one perspective to another and from that one to yet another, you see, the, uh, you need to grasp the conceptual limits of each form of consciousness right from the start, and then he goes on to say, where is it…yeah, here," flipping pages, "close to the start of the section on self-consciousness, you know, the part where he…hold on, let me find it."

"I understand," she said. "Well, I understand the general idea, or the tone, or the basic message, if it's a basic message. Past a certain point, you need to take your own understanding, your own position into account in trying to understand an object external to you."

"Yeah. Yes, yes, that's, that's right."

She knew she loved him, the way you love someone because you love them. But she couldn't remember ever having *fallen* in love. It had happened subtly or not at all. Perhaps she'd found some loophole in the system without realizing it, and now she was in a committed relationship, which meant death. She hated commitment for no reason at all, and this made her feel honest — she hated commitment without any kind of passion, or logic, as you might hate anchors, paperweights, doorstops, dumbbells. Anything that weighed her down, including her own mind at its most idiotic, she loathed, and was happy to loathe it, and it brought her no pain to admit it. She tried to explain this to him when he proposed.

"I do love you. But do I hate myself enough to wear a ring? I don't know — oh, please don't make that face. It's not because I don't love you. It's only that…"

"What? What is it?"

"I haven't got anything to offer you. As a wife. I promise. I will end up, I don't know, but I'll just float off someday if I feel constricted. Believe me. Maybe I'm being too honest."

"No, be honest. Be honest, but please, please, be kind."

"I just — I think I would hate myself if I married. If I married anyone."

"But why? What's wrong with — with us?"

"Nothing. So why change it?"

"Why indeed," and he looked at the shelves, at the guitar sitting in the corner propped up against the wall. And he ran a finger through his hair, just one finger, as though scratching his scalp, and it seemed slightly absurd: even this little gesture, meaningless except for the discomfort it suggested, made her feel braver, less tied down than ever. She felt the power of status, this true and brutal influence she might have over a hapless and kind man who just wanted to marry her, not out of flattery or lust but love, and perhaps a very human insecurity, so human that it too often went unmentioned. "Why indeed — can't you just..."

"Can't I what? Change my mind? Because you request it?"

"I only want to be with you. You don't need to marry me. But can't you at least make me understand why you hate marriage so much?"

"I don't hate marriage. I hate its symbols. I hate the ring and the veil and the dress. I hate the house and the words: husband, wife, son, daughter. Mortgage. I hate how legal it all becomes. I hate how much more serious an act of infidelity seems when it's committed in marriage. And I hate the..."

"But infidelity."

"No, nothing like that. I'm not saying anything about it, only that, you see, that I don't want that word to mean so much. It's more than a word, it's an entire cluster of bullshit. Do you understand?"

"Yes. Yes, of course I do. It's the madwoman in you, the one

I love. And not so mad at all. If you don't want to get married, then I accept that."

"Thank you. I'm sorry too. I know you really want it."

"I don't. Not anymore."

"Just because of this?"

"No. I don't know. Maybe I need to think this through on my own. I love how you make things so terribly complicated with your simplicity."

"Things need to be difficult," she misquoted Kierkegaard, "to inspire the noble-minded."

"Yes, yes, the noble-minded..." and letting the words trail behind him like reluctant pups on a leash, he left the room, the apartment, the city.

When she saw him again, three days later, she didn't ask where he'd been. This surprised him, or seemed to. He had shaved for the first time in months. He smelled clean, professional. His shirt was so beautifully ironed it might have been silk. "I'm sorry about leaving like that."

"It's fine. Come in."

"And I'm sorry about not calling."

"Come in."

"You didn't call, either."

"Did you expect me to? Did you want me to be scared?"

"No, I didn't, of course not. I just, well, I'm terrified of losing you. Which would make me feel like I'd be losing, just losing, generally."

A remark that caused her, without her wanting it, to hate him: to reconsider, in an instant, everything that they'd lived through. "Losing? Losing what, generally? Do you need me?"

"I think so. Yes, absolutely."

"I can't be with you if you need me. If you *need* to have me around."

He went quiet, and picked up the guitar in the corner, and played a chord, then another. "The diminished ninths are the most mysterious," he'd said on a happier day. She couldn't tell which chords he was playing now.

"Well, I don't — I don't *need* you like I need food."

"For Christ's sake."

"I only mean, I think, that, well."

"Well, you can't make me feel like this. It's not how I function, this pity, this constant tiptoeing around feelings. You know that. It makes me look horrible to myself, and then I'll treat you likewise."

"I don't follow. I mean, I follow, but I don't understand *you*. You know?"

In the end, she asked for time — and did not quite state, but implied as heavily as she could, that she needed the time to formulate a friendly-enough way of ending everything. "Give me a week to think about this." Then he left, and she went to bed. He took his guitar with him. Six days later she called him, tried to explain, and when he started protesting she hung up.

She met McGeeee at a book signing. Back then, it seemed to her McGeeee read an enormous amount. It turned out to be a mere book or two a month for him, but she'd bumped into him so many times at their local bookstore that she could think of no other conclusion to draw. The truth was as mundane as the fantasy it corrected: McGeeee frequented the bookstore because he was granted peace there. His father, who'd been crippled in a fishing accident on his first and only fishing trip, needed all the help he could get, but would *understand*, even with a bit of pride, if McGeeee wanted to go to the library to read to get away from his duties. But the library was too quiet for McGeeee, and so he'd go for walks before and after visiting the local bookstore.

The bookstore held a reading by a novelist she did not much care for, a man with a short black beard and grey eyebrows and the voice of an ogre. It wasn't his novels she disliked: it was the man, a gross, much too physical man with dry skin and scabby hands you might have found on someone thirty years older. As a novelist he was fine — perhaps even good. He wrote nothing of the stuff she enjoyed reading: his latest novel was a love story set in the Civil War in Spain, but, so the critics gushed, the war took a delightfully and refreshingly distant role in the story, and made room for a kind of magical realism those old Latin-American writers might have approved of. Something like that, and she couldn't be sure what else the book was about, and she didn't care, because she was only at the reading to try, for the tenth or eleventh time in as many years, to please her mother. It was her yearly attempt at a reconciliation. The visiting novelist was her mother's acquaintance, and the old woman couldn't *quite* make it because of a late-afternoon doctor's appointment on the other side of the city. So couldn't Rebecca go? Just to show her support. It would mean so much to Hugo.

"It would mean nothing to him," Rebecca said.

"You don't know that. It would help my friendship with him. He's one of my few friends left."

And that's your fault, she felt like saying; but she kept quiet, stared at her little mother in her cotton sweater and mittens (though it was warm and nobody else would have bothered to put them on) and nodded. "Fine."

"Thank you," Mildred said. "And you know, you should try your hand at writing. You'd be good at it. I'm sure of that. Maybe Hugo can give you advice."

"I don't..." But again she stopped and bit her tongue until she could feel nothing else. "I'll talk to him after the show."

Perhaps it would work this time. Perhaps Rebecca, now no longer able even to say she was in her mid-twenties, would manage a miraculous reunion with her mother over this. Maybe she could get Hugo...no, but yes, maybe Hugo the widower and Mildred the widow could... Whatever it took. If it was likely to work, or if there was even just a chance to block the outpourings of meanness and condescension of which Mildred could be so fond, then it was worth a try.

At the reading Rebecca saw and nodded at McGeeee: a nod that seemed to imply a deeper intimacy than they could really boast of. They'd spoken a few times, both of them insatiable readers (at least as far as she knew, as far as her lukewarm fantasy went), always prowling the bookshelves for something that wouldn't insult the human intelligence. He nodded back and looked away, uncomfortable, intrigued, visibly annoyed with himself for not walking over to her. So she walked to him. Here was a harmless-looking guy with whom she might be friends — almost a new concept for her: just friends, without the awkwardness of sexual tension or the implied promise of a *talk* where someone had to declare *feelings*. She had resolved, the week before, to start making friends in groups, to cut herself off from the solitude of her mind. McGeeee, the shy bookworm, might be a good place to begin building a circle of friends. And even if it went wrong — so what? It was worth trying and failing and collecting a memory.

The illusion didn't shatter when she discovered he wasn't there for the reading, but it did change. Suddenly McGeeee was the guy whose father was a cripple and whose life revolved around caring for the cripple. She sat beside him, waiting for the reading to begin — waiting, in fact, for Hugo the novelist to arrive in the first place — and listened to his story about the accident, and how he had to take care of his father but that meant he didn't get to do much else, and anyway with luck his father would start to recover soon. "I don't find it very fun," McGeeee said of his duties. "I need a break. That's why I come here."

"To read?"

"To browse. I look at the titles and try to imagine different stories based on just the words in the titles. I have peace here. It's *really* stressful dealing with a grumpy old guy who feels he's lost everything. But he likes knowing that I'm at the bookstore. It's like I'm fifteen and doing well at school. Exact same expression on his face."

It wasn't love at first sight. It wasn't much at all, except, perhaps, a vague incitement of curiosity, a bruise of interest but not quite a cut. She liked him enough, liked his hunched shoulders and lack of refinement. He didn't stammer, his hands didn't tremble, and he wasn't quite jittery enough to seem thoroughly nervous; yet he was clearly uncomfortable around her, or around people, and this was almost endearing, because in the perfect coolness she adopted in these situations, she knew *she* was doing nothing to make him uncomfortable. It was in his head. This was a link between them, maybe: this discomfort in the face of others, all as a matter of principle. They spoke, stopped, he looked around, she looked at him, he rekindled talk with "So," and made an obvious but not intentionally obvious effort to look her in the eye. *He's not creepy*, she was able to think, *but he's very slightly needy*. And despite any convictions she thought she held about men, she found herself vaguely attracted to him by the time a little man hobbled onto the platform and said into

140

the microphone that, because of unforeseen circumstances, the author would be incapable of attending —

— "Jesus Christ," his chorus of breathing went, after she'd taken him into her bed that very night, in something like a stupor, sober but not herself, not thinking it through. She'd initiated everything, had almost planned everything but hadn't: the "What do we do now?" and the conversation at a restaurant where he seemed to relax and the inter-conversational kiss she'd landed on his parted lips, then a silence, then, "Yes, okay, we'll have wine after all," and her leg under his and every single minute of their time together the thought: *I don't even know him, or care enough about him*: all of it irrelevant, since she wanted only to take him into her apartment and fuck something right out of herself, and that something, as she determined weeks later, after she'd seen him again and he'd struck her as more confident than she'd thought and she'd discovered something fiercely sexual in him that betrayed his shy demeanor, after she'd had enough time to think it through, the sudden urge to sleep with a stranger, the sheer boldness of that first kiss, a boldness she had never quite accepted in herself — that something, which she'd needed so desperately to dislodge in her mind, was her mother.

For her mother was always there somehow, lurking behind more innocuous thoughts, claws bared, eager to pounce and bite Rebecca at the throat. Something was changing in their relationship: occasionally Mildred was even tender with her daughter, only for a moment, but still — tender. And though Rebecca hadn't admitted it to herself that first night with McGeeee, her mother had been very subtly on her mind the entire time, wraithlike, observant, finally there only to imply that McGeeee was a gift, that Mother had sent Rebecca to the reading so she might find McGeeee there and wasn't that just very kind of Mother? But that was ridiculous, and Rebecca knew it. She understood, more or less, the nature of coincidence, the human inclination to pattern-finding when there were no patterns.

But what had made her so bold that night? Why had she striven to fight off her mother with casual fucking? The answer never quite arrived. She'd been on a high, an autopilot path toward sexual autonomy: as though to prove that she could very well fuck whoever she wanted, an adolescent act of rebellion. Yet there was no obvious context. She hadn't spoken to her mother about anything like sex in years. Mildred had never reproached her for whatever boyfriend she might wish to have. It seemed like an issue that simply wasn't an issue: it made no sense, that night, for her to sleep with McGeeee to rebel against her mother, since her mother wasn't there and wouldn't have minded anyway.

She carried on seeing McGeeee. He was kind, almost mysterious despite himself, and didn't ask for too much of her time: he had to take care of his father. And so Rebecca saw McGeeee, then didn't see him, and saw him again, went on with life, occasionally stopping to wonder why, or how, she'd allowed herself to set off on his trail of *settling* somewhere, of bonding with this guy, not quite falling in love but letting things go as they might, never interfering, never asking him for more than he gave, glad never to be asked herself, and things were simple. They shared some details about each other's lives, but kept just as many from each other. That worked well — and its functioning pleased her. He seemed reticent, not quite sure if he wanted to take things any further, though he cared: and she, in return, accepted the reticence and felt it likewise. They found comfort in not saying too much. She helped him find some new venetian blinds one weekend; then she stayed over to, hmm, check they worked, and they said they loved each other sometime that night, neither really imposing on the other but trying the sentiment out, each seemingly aware that the relationships you don't forget are those where both parties must be seduced into love by time, instead of out of it.

She said nothing to her mother about McGeeee, who had said nothing about Rebecca to his father. And so things remained for a few months, every threat of argument extinguished easily, every act of love more familiar and passionate and likely to place a film of sweat on their backs that left damp patches on the mattress, every weekend together not-lonely, not-false, and even, maybe, capable of making each of them forget the fundamental solitude of falling in love with somebody else.

The flux of life, with its many angles and gallops, changed forever one morning: she woke in her mother's house, aware of having dreamt *something*, but could never remember the nature of that dream, its length, its cast and plot. But something *had* happened that night. She'd fallen into a weird and viscous sleep earlier than usual, more exhausted than she'd been in years: purely, stupidly drowsy, grumpy, her bones indistinguishable from her muscles and organs, her whole body a lump of indifferent matter. She had lain on the nearest bed, not her own but her mother's, because she could not find the drive to walk up to the attic where she was meant to stay. And her mother had let her sleep, carefully aware of a change in her daughter and not keen to disturb her. Rebecca's mind, all of it, all the corners and abandoned landscapes from childhood and lovemaking and fleeting observations, all of these edges and slopes inside her folded into themselves profoundly and forever. She had fallen into the darkest and loneliest eleven hours of unmoving sleep of her life. Things changed. What these things were she couldn't say. From the very moment she woke with sunlight in her face she forgot entirely the masquerade of the night before, but knew there had been a masquerade, or a procession of cruel visions, like possession, like instinctual slivers of death. No, wait, there were still images — she'd been younger. Alone on a roof, smoking? Alone on a roof. A party. Yes, but what was it, someone had lunged at her, but...

Sun-eyed now and yawning, inexplicably distressed and afraid, she'd rubbed her face with powdery brittle hands and clenched her teeth and thought: *that was a change, I dreamed of a change*, but whatever the change was — that was impossible to tell. The secret arrangement that was her mind had shifted. A

144

chair was not where it belonged; a lightbulb had flickered on where there had been no lightbulb before. The room where she kept her thoughts was either bigger or smaller or dimmer, but *something* had changed. And she never figured it out. The sleep had transformed her. Rebecca had woken into Rebecca, but was no longer the same.

"My God, you must have been tired."

And she had been — but why? Why had she so suddenly and fatally needed to find somewhere to lie down and drop away? The sunlight — her mother's face, her mother standing there at the door, holding a glass with white slabs effervescing in its water. It was morning, it was not the same day, and as Rebecca grasped at wakefulness she turned bitterer and bitterer toward herself and her dream. Whatever the dream had been. Whatever time it was. A mood: she was in a *mood*, this was going to be a bad day, her mother took a sip from the glass and said, again, that Rebecca must have been very tired, and sat at the side of her own bed to stroke her daughter's hair, a curious tenderness.

"What did you dream," voice and sunlight, powder-eyes.

"I don't know. I was at some party. I think I jumped off a roof."

"How do you feel, then?"

"Fine. Dead."

"And you're still philosophically opposed to coffee, I suppose."

"I really don't mind coffee. I don't know why you keep saying that. What time is it?"

"Half past nine and very cold outside. The sun is misleading."

"I need to get up or I'll stay here another few days."

"You've hijacked your mother's sleeping quarters, you know."

Why so kind? Was this all it took — a night of worrying about her daughter, whose slumber was so profound she could not wake the girl even by shaking her? Was that enough to turn this woman into a caring, even a doting parent, twenty-four years after her daughter had breathed her first and somehow managed to anger her mother already? Mildred and Rebecca, too alike for their own good, you know, is what they said, and you'd agree, because Mildred and her girl Rebecca were both fierce little people with egos barely contained by those small bodies and the will-to-power of goddesses. Women who had never quite found a way to get along, except through a pleasant antagonism from which both could derive something like satisfaction. They were almost distant sisters, and each thought herself mother to the other. And now — Mildred, mother to Rebecca, was being a mother to her daughter, who, though the dread from her sleep would not be shaken off, loved it and felt warm.

"I don't know what happened. I felt this terrible need to collapse."

"And you did collapse. On my bed, of course, but that's not the gravest offense. We were supposed to watch those videos."

"They can wait, can't they?"

"I may have to send them back to Martha soon. It's important to me, Becks."

"I know."

"I watched one on my own. He was a very good-looking man in those last years. I don't know why he..." and trailed off with her fingers running along the surface of Rebecca's scalp.

"Do you..."

"Yes?"

"Regret it? You wish you'd stayed close?"

"We were never close. I never let us be close. I treated him more like an enemy than a brother."

"Because you — he *was* your enemy. In the end."

"It certainly became like that." And a strange moment of tension passed between them, a pronounced disquiet that crept into each woman's head and just as subtly disappeared. Rebecca closed her eyes and let the sunlight turn everything a blue-green mess of potentiality. Even as they spoke she knew, barely at the conscious level, of the metamorphosis of the night before. It really had been like a possession: a soul not her own had settled inside and twisted thing around, yanked at various levers, set the temple on fire. It was to last years: from that morning until the day of Mildred's funeral so much later, through Rebecca's marriage to McGeeee, the honeymoon, the settling down, the installation of routine, the wandering eyes, the colds and cramps, the pregnancy scare, the immersion in books to avoid arguments McGeeee never even suspected, the resentment toward herself and hidden from him, the long and terrible spells of missing others, the tormented intuited knowledge that even at her happiest she was suffering and couldn't explain it, through all this she felt scarred and shaken by the possession of that night. She even came to refer to it *as* possession, the demoniac takeover of her body and mind while she stayed at her mother's house one innocent evening. Rebecca, who had come only to see her mother and talk and try to make amends for trespasses for which she was supposedly responsible, found instead a totally new, numb mode of living that stayed with her those years of marriage. She'd walked into Mildred's house mostly confident and mostly tough, and the next morning walked out with an ever-deepening suspicion of horror in existence itself. And in this little moment of tension between her and her mother she had a glimpse of the newness of her situation. She *minded* it now. It bothered and scared her. Instead of the usual indifference, she felt the tension like a significant needle in the back of her neck.

When she'd near-stumbled out of bed and stretched away the most aggressive edges of anxiety, and after the ten pushups she forced herself to do every morning, she showered in her mother's bathroom and walked downstairs. Mildred was seated at the kitchen table with a few cassettes lying in front of her, spread out and unlabeled and one of them even broken in its corner. "This, now?"

"It is *important* to me, Becks."

"I know — but it's morning and..."

"And it makes you uncomfortable. Doesn't it? Doesn't it seem too much like knowing your own mother well enough that you might call her human?"

"No. It's that...I'm tired. And somehow — yes. Yes, it's

uncomfortable. You always kept so quiet about Uncle McDurrrr for so long that...well, it's..."

"We are not going to refer to him as Uncle McDurrrr," Mildred said. "I feel sorry for every McDurrrr who becomes an uncle."

"McDurrrr?"

"McDurrrr is fine. He was McDurrrr to me, and he'll be McDurrrr to you, won't he? Is that all right? God, you look strange today, Becks."

"I feel as though my sleep was...I don't know. I feel weird."

"Camomile tea," Mildred said, and rose. "The arch-nemesis of coffee."

"I don't want to fall asleep, either."

"I have other teas."

"I'm not thirsty," and Rebecca picked up the broken cassette. "This one doesn't even work, does it?"

"No."

"What was on it?"

"I don't know, exactly. More childhood footage. It's been a very long time since they transferred the videos onto these cassettes. And now with these DVDs, we'll be able to keep it going."

"You can store it on your computer. Well, you could, if you had one."

"No, thank you." Mildred's lips had subtly grown a cigarette, to which she put the flame of a match she had lit without Rebecca noticing. These little practiced tricks of habit and shame. "I don't need a computer just yet. I had you late. I'm still trying to figure out what all the little Rebecca-buttons do. Why complicate things?"

"Mother, you have never in all the time I have known you *not* tried to complicate things. That is not a criticism."

"It is, but I can let it pass. Becks, please — I have nobody else with whom I can really *sit down* and watch these. Martha's had them for years, and anyway Martha is Martha. We avoid your aunt, sweet as she is. Don't we? And who knows how long before she asks for them back?"

"If it's to help you make amends with, uh, with McDurrrr," Rebecca said.

"It's not about making amends. It's about trying to create some kind of order in the family. At least if you can *see* your uncle — if you can understand why I was so stupid, so opinionated, and how that opinionated stupidity caused me not to see my own brother for years before the final time I saw him, when he was being lowered into the ground, well..."

"But you want to watch this stuff now. This morning."

"Yes."

"All right. First, some camomile tea, please. Made by you."

"This is not a *favor* you're doing me, Rebecca. It's more than that. You never met McDurrrr and, let's face it, you don't know Martha as well as you might have wished. And that's my fault for, hmm. For not bringing you together, maybe. But we can rebuild."

"No hippie rhetoric, mother."

"No. This is more than that."

Still under the shade of the giant transformation, half-awake, sipping on her tea, Rebecca walked to the living room and waited on a couch. Mildred brought some cassettes and held one in both hands, and the hands trembled. "Thank you," she said, and put the cassette into the VCR and turned on the TV before looking at Rebecca and adding: "Thanks for indulging."

"I am interested. I'm just exhausted too."

"Watch this," Mildred said. The soundless images of children running in circles in a garden. A little girl held a bucket and said inaudible things to the air. She had eyes that drooped a little, but it was clear, from the cheekbones, that the girl was Mildred. A tiny and fragile girl surrounded by other children, everyone smiling except for her, everyone running except for her. She held her bucket and spoke, sometimes to herself, sometimes to nothing at all, and seemed unaware of anyone else.

"That's you," Rebecca said.

"Wasn't I odd?"

Then they were staring at McDurrrr. He was easy to recognize. Rebecca had seen pictures; not often, but enough times to know what he looked like: long curls on his head, the darkest eyes surrounded by profound shadows, almost suggesting mascara, a small but pretty mouth like the mouth of a young girl. McDurrrr had been a beautiful boy, confident-looking but, if you were to believe his sister, not quite as confident as he seemed. And damaged — that, too, was in his face. You couldn't see the shape of the scar, but the scar was implied in his every expression. He was looking into the camera with heroic indifference, sometimes muttering words lost to time, hostile and ironic-faced, and suddenly the camera moved and Rebecca could only see a blur of moving children.

"I don't remember, exactly. I think this was a birthday celebration."

"That was McDurrrr."

"Oh yes, that was McDurrrr."

"You need to talk about him."

"I think so. Becks, you perceptive girl, you are going to have to listen to it. But first, watch."

They watched. They saw faces not even Mildred seemed to recognize, a balloon or perhaps two, both the same degree between black-and-white and probably red at the time, and children.

"I always despised other kids."

"Even at that age?"

"Yes. I always hated being surrounded by children. And when I reached adolescence, I suppose other adolescents became the problem. And so on. You were like that yourself, you know."

Rebecca knew. "How does it feel, seeing these — seeing all of this past?"

"Very ugly. Inside. It feels ugly and wrong."

Instead of asking, Rebecca chose to interpret; and at once saw in her choice a decisive difference between her relationship with her mother and the relationships of most children with Mother. And it was the first time since the previous night's possession that she had *proof* or something like it: proof that something had *changed* inside her, that she would never again behave as she would have behaved without that demonic night. Had this been a normal day, Rebecca would have pressed for more. But she didn't care what Mildred meant, exactly; or at least didn't want confirmation of anything. Mildred felt ugly inside and wrong when she saw footage from her youth. Why ask why? Why not just settle for silence, and space for misunderstanding, and a tiny gap between what Mildred had meant and what Rebecca had assumed her to mean? And what she thought her mother had meant was that she felt a literal ugliness, a total uncompromising wrongness in herself. That was all. There was no need to ask what had brought the ugliness on and what made things wrong. No need for discussion and exposition, as in plays, novels, the stories people liked to tell to explain their inexplicable actions.

"There's a lot of footage here," Rebecca said, motioning to the cassettes on the table.

"I didn't even know handheld cameras were a thing back then."

Perhaps this was the wrong thing to say — perhaps, as the tiny twitch that ran through her mother's body suggested, she had been meant to ask *why* Mildred felt ugly and wrong. But Mildred recovered, and shrugged the question off with, "There were telephones, too, you know."

"But handheld cameras?"

"Not quite the same kind of *handheld* you'd see now, certainly, but you could rent out a camera for the day. I didn't grow up in the age of daguerreotypes or telegrams, you know."

"I see."

Mildred clenched a fist, sank it gently into her own chin. "Becks, it's important to me that you see these videos. I want you to get a sense of our history, our family."

"That sounds like something you'd have laughed at, a few years ago."

"I know."

"Then the change is because, what, you feel I don't know the family well enough? That was because you never let us get too close to Aunt Martha and the others."

"No," Mildred said, looking at the ceiling. "I don't blame you for anything. Perhaps it's more *me* trying to recover some of the past. I want to know what you know about where you come from. Becks, we have never *talked* about your roots, my roots. And I feel I mistreated you a few times, didn't handle situations well enough."

"Like what?"

"Like when Uncle Gerald came with Mary and Richard and... well, that summer. I feel I didn't handle it correctly, I overreacted, and I have to talk to you about it."

"Mother..." Rebecca, suddenly very awake and on the verge of breaking out in a sweat, raised her hand as if to stop the conversation. "Why now?"

"No. Listen. It was wrong of me to act so outraged. You were only young, experimenting, but..."

A short silence full of sunlight.

"You caught me kissing a cousin when I was fifteen and you acted like I'd been fucking him," Rebecca said. "You humiliated me, humiliated him, and Uncle Gerald, and Aunt Mary, and everyone else who knew what had happened, as if something had *happened*. I've tried to get over this and now you bring it up, what, a decade later? Why?"

"Because — damn it, listen to me, please. Because we haven't worked things out, I know it's all a bit tense, and...I'm reevaluating, I'm thinking it through and trying to — well, I'm trying..."

"Don't you think we could have let it rest?" Rebecca went on, more agitated than she wanted to be. "Couldn't we have accepted it as a dumb thing I did among many dumb things as a fifteen-year-old and not ever mention it again? Does it need bringing up?"

"It doesn't need bringing up," Mildred said, "but I'm trying to apologize for how I behaved. I got hysterical, and maybe if... if you understand *why* I..."

"You sat me down with Rich and Uncle Gerald and Aunt Mary and *insisted* on talking about it as some sort of..."

"I know, I remember."

"Some sort of crime!"

"I know."

"I'd never kissed a boy, mother. It was only...it was almost a game. Just because we could and we were old enough to want to try it."

"I know, damn it." And Mildred pointed at the television, where a tiny version of herself was speaking mutely into the camera again. "That's what this is about."

"How? Why are you making me watch these videos?"

"Because for once in our lives we should *talk*."

Rebecca sat staring at her mother: the early wrinkles, the tiny nose. For the first time in her life, she saw her mother as an old woman: a suddenly old and frail and greying figure reaching for a pack of cigarettes in a drawer and taking out the last cigarette in the pack with a trembling hand. The lighter, the flame, the smell of burning, smoke coming out like sludge from the woman's tiny nose.

"Talking," Mildred said. "The one thing we cannot seem to do."

"Perhaps."

"You don't want to talk about that summer, fine. It was only one of many things I wanted to mention. I...I was hoping I could tell you about the past, our family — *your* family — but I suppose it can wait. I don't want to discuss it when we're both..."

"What?"

"Stressed out like this."

"It's fine, mother."

"No. I'm not fine."

And the old lady sat there silently puffing on the cigarette, looking at the back of her other hand and not crying, never crying, but brooding and folding inward. A full minute, then two, passed. Rebecca tried not to look at her mother. Then, brusquely, almost jerking upwards, Mildred was on her feet. "I need to go for a tiny walk. Let me clear my head, Becks. I'll be back in twenty minutes." And she left the room. The sound of the front door closing.

Rebecca's first instinct was not to move: to remain there, seated just as she was, not even moving her arm to wipe the drop of sweat forming at her temple. But that was too dramatic. She couldn't think. She entered her room for the first time since the day before, dressed herself as quickly as she could, tied her hair in a ponytail. Her mother had slept there, while Rebecca had been possessed by whatever it was the night before. On the unmade bed were some papers, photographs. She recognized herself as a child holding a cat, as a teenager washing a car. Whatever had brought on her mother's contemplative, serious mood, she'd probably get a whiff of it here, in these pictures, these papers. She looked through them without moving anything but her hands and eyes. Pictures of her father — a few of them, before his stroke. She barely remembered him, didn't miss him, didn't feel his absence. Pictures of her Uncle Gerald, holding the same cat, the cat fatter now, Gerald smiling but tired. Her Aunt Martha, young, sitting in someone's kitchen, raising a cup of something. That was the only picture of Martha. No pictures of her grandmother, whom she'd always called Granny Grumps, but had never got to know meaningfully before death struck.

(Why had she called her Granny Grumps? Nobody had ever spoken of the lady as grumpy, or, indeed, as anything but kind; even Rebecca's mother, who did not speak to Granny Grumps and had been reluctant to let Martha take Rebecca to see her granny, had said a kind thing or two about her.) The papers: drawings Rebecca had made as a child on napkins. Scribbles she couldn't make out. An adult's handwriting she couldn't make out either. On a sheet of brown, still scented paper, a letter from Martha to her sister, Rebecca's mother. She read the first paragraph, then put it down. On another sheet, another letter, this one from Rebecca to her mother, a thirteen-year-old Rebecca wishing her mother a happy birthday.

This was intentional: why else would her mother have left everything here, now? Had she fallen asleep in this mess, trying to formulate her thoughts while Rebecca, too, slept, to ensure the talk she planned for them went smoothly? Was all of this a way of forcing her daughter to confront the terrible inadequacy of their relationship? She carried on rummaging through the letters, the pictures, the plane ticket stubs: Arizona. Paris. Paris, a year later. And she found a letter from her mother: *from* Mildred, yet in Mildred's possession. An unsent letter; and, in fact, as Rebecca now saw, an unfinished letter. The paper had been folded over so many times it looked like a cube, but it hadn't been thrown away, so Rebecca read what was there.

Gerald,

Thank you for the book and the card. I read it (the book, but yes, the card too...) and I enjoyed it. It hasn't changed my mind — why would it? — but I appreciated your effort. I hope you'd agree that I've been far less hostile to all that stuff these last few years. It won't surprise you, probably, that I'm not quite converted by the book, but whereas twenty years ago I'd have looked on it with all the condescension I could muster, now I just let it slide. It still seems a bit kooky to me — this talk of energy and life force and meditation for the sake of universal harmony. But you chose the right book to try and win me over; it wasn't at all a stupid book, although, if I can be honest, it still struck me as immensely naïve. But then I don't meditate and I don't see evidence of a total and beautiful life force flexing the muscles of the cosmos. I wonder if some of us are just doomed not to find any intrinsic beauty in things. Not that I want to sound gruesomely cynical to you. You know I'm glad you've found your balance; seeing you recover from your more depressed days is wonderful. I'm surprised and not surprised at the same time that it took this kind of thinking, this elevation of optimism into a cosmic principle, to help you get through the dark. Whatever it took, though. I'm glad you've stuck around.

There are things that I feel about all of that — that darkness — that I wanted to share with you about a year and a half ago, when you came over with Amanda. You'll probably recall it as the time Rebecca spilled juice exactly everywhere we didn't want it to be spilled: Amanda's dress, my papers, the carpet. Rebecca falls over a lot. I'm starting to wonder about that. But — that was a very bad time for you in your life, I know, and I knew it back then, which was why I didn't treat you to my morbid views. But reading the book you sent

And there the letter ended. Without pausing for half a second, without wanting even to consider the implications of what she'd been reading, she looked around for another cube of folded paper. She found two. The first read:

I am trying to make myself sound far more at peace with myself than I am. Let me admit that. Things have been strange. I can't stop thinking about McDurrrr. So little of my understanding of McDurrrr makes any sense — I blinded myself, willingly, from the moment we cut ties until the moment I heard he went off. I never wanted to accept that I had done more to hurt him than anything else; though he hurt me in many more ways. I resented him, found his faith hypocritical, considered him spoilt. But I was spoilt too. And Martha was always in the background, being good, minding her own. It infuriated me too.

The second:

I always knew, of course, though I used to pride myself on not acknowledging it, that you and McDurrrr were closer than he and I ever were, though yes, yes, but aside from that…I always knew it, always resented it, pretended it wasn't the case, pretended I despised him, so forth forever until the day he just decided to fuck off without giving anyone a heads up. And I have been thinking about all this recently because I get these glimpses of a better way to do things sometimes — mere glimpses, they only last so long, and I have to act on them while they're still useful. And so recently I, what can I call it, I suppose it was a glimpse: I glimpsed (writing that over and over makes the word appear so strange) the face of my brother in the mirror. And I don't mean it symbolically, though of course the symbolism will invite itself and find its nest there. I literally saw, for a mere second, a brutal shard of a second, McDurrrr's face in the mirror as I was walking past it. I saw it: handsome and defiant and adolescent. It terrified me, of course, but beyond that it only made me very sad. Ashamed of myself. Sometimes I read the letter he sent me, the very last one, before we lost all touch, and I feel the deepest shame I know. And you two were so close that I never felt comfortable trying to help you when you spiraled out of control. You understand this? I know a good deal of it was to do with him going. How could I, who sometimes hated but never quite managed not to love my brother, and who had pushed him away so much, try to comfort you when you were upset about him? And why couldn't I just — cry, perhaps, or show something like misery? But I caught a glimpse of another face recently, let's call it the face of practical sense, though I nauseate myself this way…I can't help thinking that you and I need to sit down and talk about all of this. I have a daughter, I am a widow, I have few friends, and I feel shredded to bits every time I think of how cruel I was to McDurrrr, and how cruel he was to me, how useless I have always been with family, how selfish, how unfair.

Staring now at these words, vaguely understanding something she couldn't express, understanding it maybe in her most inaccessible puddles of mind, Rebecca wept. It was the first time in years — the first time since she'd left Romania after falling in love, perhaps. She couldn't remember, and tried to remember as she wept. Her mother wasn't back; Rebecca stood and looked at herself in the mirror and, knowing she wouldn't be able to talk to her mother like this, picked up her bag, left the house and drove away.

With McGeeee, life slowed down. He always woke up before her, prepared the breakfast table, and went for a walk. When she managed to pry her eyes open, he was back in bed with her, but dressed, awake, thoughtful. They weren't married: they didn't speak of love very much, didn't acknowledge to each other the creeping possibility of marriage, didn't even speak of the future. She often spent more time at his apartment than she'd anticipated, one night, then three and four, and only returned to her own little studio to make sure it hadn't burned down. The routine she'd established with McGeeee was convenient — the pressure was off, he never upset her, even when she secretly wished to get a bit upset, and she, in return, kept him company, and visited his father with him. McGeeee's duties to the old man never wavered. Every day he drove to the nursing home and spoke with his father for an hour, asked the nurses how things were going, chatted with the head nurse, and then drove off and did part time work wherever he found it. Rebecca soon discovered he didn't quite need money: his mother's death had left him and his father with a sum of money Rebecca could barely make sense of, though it wasn't even a question of millions. When he found work as a manager for an elevator maintenance company that treated him like any other employee, McGeeee still didn't need the money: he worked because he wanted to, because his father had stopped talking to anyone and every day sank into profounder senility, and McGeeee wanted a distraction. Rebecca learned quickly that for him, everything was a distraction — but from what, she never managed to understand.

Still, life slowed down and turned comfortable for both of them. She wrote occasional articles for a local magazine, and was bored with them before they were even in print. He went for walks, kept to himself when he could, tried to take up jogging a few times, asked her if she wanted a dog and didn't insist when she said she wasn't comfortable around pets. "Animals need to run around."

"A dog could run around here."

"It's a big commitment."

"Yes."

And they left it at that and didn't buy the dog, but the question of commitment had been raised now. It festered in their minds, clawed its way into their conversations, and eventually, when Rebecca realized she really did mean it when she told him she loved him, and would miss him painfully if she lost him, she brought up marriage. They didn't decide anything — they couldn't yet. She'd never introduced McGeeee to her mother, out of fear and pride and a suspicion that she'd disapprove simply because she could. She barely saw her mother these days, alone or otherwise. It took a conversation with Rita, the only friend from childhood whose name she could even remember, and the only friend she trusted enough to discuss McGeeee with, before she changed her mind. "You're a private person, sure," Rita had said. "That doesn't mean you have to be paranoid. Especially with your own mother."

"You know what she's like."

"Yes. And I know she'd want to meet McGeeee."

"I feel awkward about him somehow. I love him, but I don't want anyone to know I love him — especially her."

"You don't want anyone to know you love anyone."

"Probably true."

"Why?"

"No idea."

"Try again."

"I don't know. Love feels…"

"Feels what?"

"Wrong to talk about, I suppose."

"With your own mother, though."

"My own mother above all else. I can't stand to talk about this. With her. Ever since I slammed the door in her face when she…"

"Slammed the door?"

"Metaphorically."

"When she what?"

"When she tried to open up. And for whatever childish reason I couldn't handle it. I froze. I've been feeling weird since that day. That morning I woke up and I — what can I call it — I felt I'd been fucked by a demon. I felt wrong. Like some kind of morning fever. I've felt wrong ever since. And I think I was still reeling from waking up like that, and I acted badly. I know I hurt her feelings. She really was trying to open up."

"Fucked... by a demon. An incubus."

"No, not like that, not really. Nothing supernatural, yet somehow it does feel supernatural. All these months I've been wrestling with a feeling of *wrongness*, like something's twisted, a knot inside me that won't get undone. Ever since I woke up that morning. In my mother's bed, because I'd felt so...exhausted. I couldn't even make it to my own bedroom. She had to sleep where I was meant to sleep. I found all sorts of letters and — how the hell do I explain it? Letters, pictures, of me, of the family. I think she'd fallen asleep going through them all. And I saw a few scraps of letters she'd never sent to my uncle. I sensed pain in them. Sensed, no, I *saw* the pain in them, and I was overwhelmed, I left while she was out and, you see, we haven't talked about any of that since. The *one* time in my life when my mother, out of the blue, tries to make up for lost time with me and I..."

"So let her in now, you fool. Tell her about McGeeee. Let them meet each other."

"I want to. But I don't want to at all. I mean it, I don't feel like I'm myself since I woke up that morning. I do things a little differently. Or maybe that's not it. I *feel* things differently. Like everything tastes different when you're sick. I get this dream sometimes, the same series of visions, and it comes back to me: the ambiguous feeling. Just an ambiguous feeling. A chunk of unspecific emotion. Really, a block of..."

"About what? A feeling of what?"

"Hell if I know. Not sadness, not despair, not joy. I just feel the feeling itself as an extra layer of feeling. Does that even, no, of course not. But it links back to this dream I have sometimes. I keep having it, more and more. A vision of a city. An old couple, not elderly but *old*, not graceful, not *wise* and experienced, just, you know, too grown up and incapable of anything but slow movements and slow conversations. I can't hear what they're saying. I somehow feel it's me and McGeeee, but it's never clear. This old couple walking arm in arm through the streets for days without rest. No sleep or pauses for food. The city dark, filled with ice, and shadows, reclining here, appearing elsewhere to darken everything over again. Hard to explain, just these gusts of wind pummeling the faces of those who have been... condemned, maybe, to walk forever in these streets. Whispers, occasional whistling from the darker alleys. You get the picture. Black and grey and dirt and ash, the smell of damp clothes everywhere, the smell of sad forgotten death. I keep thinking: wake up, wake up. The whole city anonymous and indifferent to itself, negligible, tucked away. Inside me. The pavement everywhere a bed of dead cigarettes. Television screens that once flickered. Subway trains stopped halfway there. The entrances to apartment buildings cracked or simply gone. Cans, lighters, posters peeling away, debris from other things nobody remembers. And people not bothering to fall down and die. Everyone wandering the streets forever, the sun never rising, never setting. Clouds and the threat of hail. This old couple turning a corner. And always: is this me and McGeeee?"

"Rebecca."

"Is it? Why am I having this dream over and over and over? I've written it down, I've described it on paper just as I described it to you. It's *debris* from things nobody remembers. That's what this is. Debris."

"Forget the dream. Let her meet McGeeee. It's like you're

fighting with yourself and both sides want the same thing. You want her to meet him. Just let her."

"You think that's what it is?"

"I think so. I think as soon you've allowed yourself to be let into your mother's intimacies, and she reciprocates, yeah, I think you'll feel better. Forget that dream. It's just an apocalypse in your head. It won't change anything."

It still took her some weeks before Rebecca, in her fortnightly phone call to her mother (fortnightly, now, because of the sudden change in her mother's tone whenever they spoke, and because of Rebecca's apprehension toward the whole situation), mentioned her boyfriend, as if in passing, not pausing to wait for Mildred's reaction. That reaction was a simple "Hmm," and Mildred only brought up "the boyfriend" later on in the conversation.

"So this boyfriend is why I almost never hear from you?"

"No, mother."

"Is he nice?"

"He's very nice," and left it at that.

When, finally, she brought McGeeee to her mother's house, the first thing she noticed was the smell of cigarettes: that rancid odor like mild piss floating through the air, lurking around the ashtrays on every table and counter crammed with butts and dead lighters. She kept silent and kept her gaze on McGeeee, who winced a little as he took off his coat and folded it around his arm. Mildred pointed at a wooden hook in the wall. "Hang your coat there," she said, and watched him do it. "It's nice to meet you, McGeeee. Becks is very quiet about her love life, you know. This is unprecedented."

He looked in Rebecca's direction, but not quite at Rebecca. "Glad I qualify for the role."

"Let's go to the living room."

"Mother, can we open a window? You're smoking a lot. Since when is it this bad?"

Mildred said nothing but led McGeeee to a couch in the living room.

"Mother."

"I'm smoking a lot, yes, dear. McGeeee, something to drink?"

And that was the end of the conversation: never mind that smoking was a cancerous hobby, and that, ultimately, cancer would indeed kill her. Never mind — because who cared. Her mother wouldn't listen. So Rebecca sat there and listened to what small talk the others could generate without her, and she frowned, then tried not to frown, interjected occasionally when she felt someone grow awkward. Mildred asked no questions of a very personal kind. McGeeee gave no personal answers. From Mildred's "Rebecca told me you work with a company that makes elevators" there followed a "Yes, that's right" from McGeeee and a tiny second of silence before McGeeee, taking the lead, launched into a short anecdote to explain why he had decided to, uh, work there, because his father was ill and — Rebecca sitting and digesting everyone's words, trying to sort out pleasantries and banalities from what she thought was sincere probing and offering, noting which details McGeeee left out and which he considered too important not to share, scrutinizing the expressions on her mother's face, feeling a widening patch of sweat under each arm, wondering: *am I even needed here, shouldn't I let them fend for themselves, is this even a war, am I nervous beyond any justification?*

She needed to walk. No need to be there, to babysit. "Mother, I'll be right back," she said, squeezed McGeeee's hand, stood, walked out of the living room. Upstairs. Her head weighing everything down. She closed the door and lay on her bed, where she'd spent her entire childhood falling asleep and waking up and dreaming about whatever she had dreamed about before she'd grown into *this*, whoever she was, and she closed her eyes. But now she'd fall asleep like this. She'd been in that position ten seconds before she was up again and she went to the bathroom, her bathroom, where her things were still stored in little drawers. Her mother hadn't touched anything. And Rebecca had never stopped to consider it, and knew now that she should, but refused to. Not now. She had suspected, correctly, that her period was starting. Hadn't brought anything with her. She looked through the drawers, found old soaps and bottles of shampoo long empty but kept like any other item of value in case *something*.

Her mother, perhaps, had tampons. Or perhaps not. They didn't talk about menopause because they talked about nothing. Worth trying, anyway. She walked to Mildred's room and looked in that bathroom for tampons, pads, but they weren't in any obvious place. A single toothbrush, a tiny green case for contact lenses. An orange bottle of pills: a brand name she recognized. At first she associated the name of the medication with herpes. But that couldn't be right. That was something else. This was a kind of antidepressant. From the Prozac family. That was it. The kind of thing her old musician boyfriend had taken: "A way of not going too far down."

"Down what?"

"You'd laugh if I called it an abyss. But it's an abyss."

"I'm not laughing."

Because Rebecca hadn't ever taken such medication. And he swallowed that little pill every morning. Not to go too far down that abyss. Now Rebecca looked at the white pills turned orange by the bottle and the light, and nothing: thought nothing, breathed almost without inhaling, deflated, flattened out. She focused on the medication, what a single pill suggested. Progress, medical and human. Emotional progress. This was what the older worlds hadn't been cunning enough to create. Capsules of very gradual progress. "You take the first one," the musician had said, "and you take the next one, and so on, and over time, over a couple of months, your brain gets used to it, starts to behave in a way you didn't think it would. You're stable. You have some control.

Apart from the occasional judgment from someone who *doesn't believe in pills*, and wants you to be aware of this, you don't worry so much about people. You get numb, I suppose." Numb, yes, you suppose, numb and impotent, as I recall. Sometimes impotent and sometimes drowsy and, yeah, sometimes *better*, statistically likelier not to overreact about things. I remember. And now my mother needs this. She is receiving the help. Itty bitty progress. My depressed and lonesome mother.

Depressed, but why — what took you from grouchy to hopeless? The pills rolling around in the bottle rolling around in her hand, a sudden cramp Rebecca's wrist, now a twitch, the bottle falling into the sink. She picked it up again and the rolling resumed. You grow up every time you realize your mother is only human and was always only human. And after enough growing up over the years, you want those reminders of her humanity to stop. You're enough of an adult now, you get it. But it keeps happening: it used to be as simple as hearing her admit she was wrong about something. Then you'd get into arguments and she seemed far more shaken than you were. Now it's your mother living alone in the house you left and she has anti-depressants in the bathroom and every inch of this place stinks like cigarette smoke. And leaves you to discover these things on your own.

Her first impulse — the impulse of narcissism — was to blame herself, or to find herself somehow implied in this. The thought of those pills sliding down her mother's throat. The loneliness in the house. Because Rebecca hadn't been there, hadn't found a way into her mother's confidences, and didn't care enough (pretended not to care enough) to keep trying. Her mother's life amounted to little more than cigarettes and memories she didn't share with her only child, and the child never pushed hard enough. She was old enough now to take charge and change things: tell her mother to trust her, to let down her guard. Just as her mother had tried too. Yes. Neither of them ever ready at the same time. One would push and the other just recoiled, and months later the roles were switched. Never good enough timing. When mother wished to talk, child wished for peace. Then child wanted to be serious with mother and mother crumbled under the pressure. And now this: mother feeling totally alone, widowed for years, child old enough to live on her own, and introducing her man *officially*, old enough, then, to take the lead and sit mother down and say: "Look, we've been tiptoeing around *something* for years and if we don't talk about it now, we may never do it." To which the only reply should be: "Yes. We need to talk." And they would talk. It would all boil down to an infinite amount of nothing. Knots to be undone. That was it.

She walked back downstairs and found McGeeee pacing around the kitchen on his cellphone. Mildred was running water into the kettle. "Everything okay?"

"Yes."

"McGeeee's got a call from work, I think."

She looked at McGeeee, who nodded quietly and frowned and continued to pace.

"No coffee for you, I imagine," Mildred said.

"No coffee for me. Mother," Rebecca lowering her voice, "how was it?"

A whisper: "A nice conversation. He seems perfectly pleasant."

"That's it?"

At first Mildred gave no reply. She placed the kettle on the stove and took out two mugs from the cupboard and opened a glass jar full of powdered coffee and smiled. It was joyless. When McGeeee had paced away into the living room, she said, "I'm simply glad you're well and happy. If you want my approval, you have it."

"What's wrong?"

"What do you mean?"

"Look. It's, I don't know, it's time, maybe. We should talk about the future now. I'm bound to be engaged to this guy soon enough. I'm glad you like him. But there's more than that."

"There's more than that in what sense?"

"Mother."

"I know, Becks."

"I was looking for tampons in your bathroom."

"You won't find any."

"I know. I found the anti-depressants though."

"Rebecca, that's none of your business."

"I know."

"Is this what you want to talk about? It really isn't any of your business."

"I know."

Mildred's mouth was trembling gently. "Becks, I've tried to talk to you about things. You know I have. But the last time I made a serious effort, you walked away. Those videos. It was important that you see them. You didn't even let me explain why. And..."

"I understand."

"Now I don't even know if it's the right thing to do. To talk to you about these things."

"You have to."

"I do not have to." A kindling of anger in Mildred's eyes.

"You don't have to. But let's try."

"Easy, yes, when you're the one initiating things."

McGeeee walked back into the kitchen. He shrugged — the first time Rebecca had seen him clearly affecting a shrug — and held up his phone. "I may have a problem. This was supposed to be my day off, but one of our technicians got his foot crushed while fixing an elevator and I have to go in."

"Crushed?" Mildred took the whistling kettle off the stove and poured water into the mugs.

"Pretty likely he's going to lose the foot, apparently." He looked at Rebecca, who could think of nothing but his departure, *untimely and annoying* though it certainly was for everybody, so she could sit and talk with her mother. She barely remembered him or knew who he was: her body tingled and rolled under itself with anxiety. Let him go. She'd join him later. Anything but a formal introduction now, anything but this false being polite, this here-mother-meet-my-boyfriend idiocy. She'd found a way in.

"You have to go?" she said, casual as possible.

"I don't want to. I have to. I'm very sorry."

"Unfortunate timing," Mildred said. "But we got to talk, at least."

Go away, go away. Rebecca took McGeeee by the hand for a few seconds. "You'll let me know when you're on your way home?"

"Yes."

"Don't worry. It's important that you go. You can hang out with my mom another time."

Even Mildred managed a contortion of a real smile. "It was a pleasure."

And after an exchange of goodbyes Rebecca led her man to the door and kissed him as patiently as she knew how and watched him drive away. She stood on the driveway looking at the gravel in its variations, its cracks, its shades of black and grey. She could feel her mother's gaze on her, but didn't turn around: only stood and looked down. "You want to talk, then?"

Her mother's voice back to its uncomplaining monotone: "I suppose we have to."

HATRED OF MOTHERHOOD

She knew, and had known for years, that there were no origins. Pull back the curtain and you will find another curtain. Masks masking masks. There was no *original* anything, because a person always imitates another person imitating other people. It was a founding principle in her understanding of things. You took on this part of your father or his stand-in, and this of your mother, and this of the schoolyard bully, this of that, until you had completely lost track of what debt was owed to whom, if you ever had bothered to keep track. You fooled yourself into thinking that you were yourself, and the world was a mess of other things external and often dangerous. The origin was you, and you were original. The lie was convincing, and it turned you into a delicate and dangerous invention. But by then you'd forgotten how to merge with the world.

Her mother never insisted on the delusion. Mildred, for all her flaws as a parent, had managed somehow, if it wasn't just all down to hereditary luck, to transmit to Rebecca the subtlety of thought that had made both of them so complicit in each other's misery for so long. Mother and daughter both understood the debt they had incurred to nobody in particular, the debt that goes with coming to life in a world populated by humans who sometimes do bad things, and sometimes do good things, and convince themselves that the badness or goodness of their actions depends on some original judgment. First Mildred, and then Rebecca: all the previous generations condensed in individual women who knew the implication of living with others without a God or an absolute. If there was no origin, it was impossible to convince the world of that. There was no original world, either — no one source of conflict that could be eliminated, no single divine pronouncement to turn love into something essential to the universe, or even into a recurring pattern in its fabric. Yet now, Rebecca wanted only to try, and try again, and keep trying, to impose something like love onto the shapeless thing they had constructed: to force herself to be kind to her mother, truly kind, not *nice* or *tolerant* or *understanding* but terribly, unreasonably *kind*; and she hoped the violence would be returned in full. There would be no progress otherwise, and if she didn't believe in progress as a goal of history, she still dared to work for it now, here, with her mother.

They were sitting in the living room, arms folded, staring at each other.

"You think it's a bad idea to talk now?"

"No," Mildred said. "Perhaps it's never going to be a *good* idea, but now, well, maybe now is as good a time as it will ever be."

"Mother, I'm a quarter of a century old. I know it's nothing, but it's something too. I'm not young enough to believe things will just work out if I'm patient enough."

"You have all sorts of other foolish beliefs, Becks. We all do, no matter how old we get."

"You understand what I mean."

"Yes."

"Can we try to work this out?"

"I don't even know what *this* is, Rebecca. I don't know. We've had these conversations before. I've begun them all, recently. At least until today. You really make me feel as though I'd be better off not wasting my time with any of it. You make me feel repellent. I try to get close to you, and you find that intimidating. Maybe I'm heavy-handed about it, but that's not a good reason to dismiss me."

"I don't dismiss you. I just don't get you."

Mildred reached for a cigarette.

"Why are you smoking so much?"

"I smoke a great deal. Leave it at that, please."

"Why are you taking those meds?"

"There's nothing wrong with taking antidepressants."

"I didn't say there was. I just want to know why."

"Because I don't feel well, Becks."

The cigarette let out its first sigh of smoke.

"And why don't you feel well? What, why don't you ever seem to feel well?"

"I have grown into a cynical and lonely old woman," Mildred said. "To you, I'm your mother. To me, I'm *me*, experiencing the world at every moment like everyone else, and I'm unhappy. I regret things. I know things I wish I didn't. Your father has been gone for years, and every week it seems I find a new way of accusing myself of having been terrible with him."

"Were you unfaithful?"

"I didn't get married for the right reasons."

"You didn't love him?"

"Of course I loved him. If love were enough, marriage would be easy."

"Mother," Rebecca said, and tried to control her voice, to channel it into sympathy. "Just talk to me."

"I've known you for twenty-five years, my baby. I've talked to you plenty. I breastfed you, taught you words, drove you to school. I watched you get fiercer and less complacent every year. I let you do what you felt was right most of the time, and I let you get angry at me, insult me, ignore me when you started behaving something like a woman instead of a little girl. Your birth was the end of a life for me and the start of a very different one. But I did have that life before you. I think you forget that."

"I don't understand. What happened before I was born, then? What's the point?"

"What happened was that I grew up much as you did, felt similar feelings no doubt, grew angry with my own mother, argued with people to assert myself. I made some trivial mistakes, and some very serious ones. I had mild infatuations and very deep adolescent loves, eventually. There was a whole universe before I gave birth to you, and I've spent years trying to find a balance between nostalgia and repulsion and gratitude and shame."

"Over what?"

"Becks."

"Tell me." Rebecca kept her eyes on her mother's face, as though to force it to stare back at her. It was a face of rigid nothingness. The skin concealed a blank.

"Tell you what?"

"Tell me."

"I've tried to get there. You can't even imagine, because you don't know the very basic facts. But I've tried to tell you, or at least to set the conditions for it to be possible someday."

"Just say it. What happened?"

"There is no just saying it, Becks."

"Why?"

"Because what I am trying to express is an entire chunk of what I am."

"What *are* you then?"

"I'm your mother. Which is why it's doubly impossible to explain."

"What does this have to do with me? What don't I know?"

"Stop *asking* me and let me get there."

The sunlight dimmed. Outside, a thin, numb grey had settled across the sky.

"Do you want me just to shut up?"

"No," Mildred said. "Only let me gather my thoughts as I speak." She had finished her cigarette. She smoked even as she talked. Soon a new one was in her mouth. "Let me try to find a way to get this somehow to make sense."

"I'm listening."

"Wait until I have something to say. I'm going to mess it up the first few times." A smile like a twitching dead frog.

"Mother."

"It's just not easy to, well, to say that what you are, what you've been, these twenty-five years, it...shouldn't be changed. It can't be changed. But the past is so brutal when you accept its power, when you look at yourself and see only the work of generations of not knowing. I was the culmination of that process, once. McDurrrr was the eldest, really, since Martha wasn't our sister by blood. And McDurrrr, once, had been the culmination, too, the latest and youngest in a very long line of human beings tied by blood and effort and so much time. Then I came along, fresher and younger than McDurrrr. Suddenly I was the limit to the centuries, the millennia, of breeding and starved suffering that life flickered through in all our ancestors."

"And now me."

"I suppose it's a bit of a digression before I've even started telling you the story. But maybe you could say the story *begins* with a digression. So yes, you, eventually. But before you, me: the youngest and the most resilient and furious, they said among themselves, to your grandmother. They told me, even. I was the *angriest*, as though at last the rage of centuries had found its seat in my voice. I don't know who our ancestors were; not really. I don't know, not past the names of your great-great-grandparents. I've forgotten. But we were always like this. Not cursed, not doomed, except by time. Only struggling to rage against our lives. And I was the peak of it all, the one who raged aloud. Your grandmother and I had a relationship much like ours, mine and yours. The same missed opportunities. The same unsaid."

"The same mystery?"

"You find me mysterious?"

"Not that. Yes, but it's not what I meant. The mystery that you're trying to explain to me. I feel there's a revelation coming. You're killing time."

"Becks." Smoke curling like earrings around the air. "For once that we have time and are actually seizing it, don't think

I'm trying to kill it. I want you to understand things as I think I understood them."

"What were the things?"

"Ah, damn," Mildred suddenly biting her lip, eyes accommodating tears, "damn, damn, yes, I know. The things. What happened, you want to know. Why the big secret. Why the…the…"

"Mother," Rebecca's voice cracking, too, from the sheer baffling suddenness of it, "what is it?"

"I just want to explain to you why I, or you, why *you* never met your uncle. Why I never again saw him. Why that summer with — those moments of silence between us that lasted so many weeks at a time…."

"He was a priest," Rebecca trying to stay calm, trying for grace. "He stood for everything you hated about the weakness of people, the institutions that ruled them. You had principles and he had his and at the time you thought it was all just irreconcilable so you went your ways. Then you reached out to, to *him* and discovered he was dead. I know the story. Your temper. Your arrogance, and his. You've explained this before."

"The explanation was a lie and a lie and a lie."

"A lie to cover what?"

The tears were drying up. Mildred's voice rolled over into a terrifying murmur. "To cover the nakedness of love, Becks. I loved him very much. Your uncle was a good man. He was kind and he cared about people. He was my *brother*: I saw him turn into the man you would have loved, I watched the transformation: from confused and insecure budding intellectual to a real brain, a true heart. He was what a biographer would have called iconoclastic, maybe. All over the place, thinking ten thoughts at once, desperate to understand what the world was. Angry, too, sometimes. Prone to — violence isn't the word, but — resentment, a brief flaring of indignation here and there. He confused himself. I wish you could have known him, sometimes.

And other times, no, I'm just glad things ended as they did."

"Ended how? What happened?"

"What happened…"

"Mother."

"What happened just, I can't even, what happened simply happened. Becks, you can't know it, you can't even begin to see."

"What?"

"The damned — the — the force of our damned family. The institutions, Becks. You'll understand. Just give me time to say it aloud."

"You loved him?"

"Of course I loved him."

"As a lover?"

It wasn't silence. She had heard her own question, faint, crowded out by tiny screams. A loudening of violence. Blood-soaked voice asking mother if uncle was lover and mother not answering because both deafened by shrieks and howls. Shrieks and agony stirring everything in her, in her mother. Bodies disconnected from themselves. Thoughts linked by nothing. All she heard there, now, while Mildred tried to deny and confirm and stumbled over the yesnoyesnoyes, was the screaming, pitches too high for people, too low, an absolute clash of voices between her ears. "As a…" Rebecca or Mildred speaking, "as a lover…" while the liars and the thieves and the butchers fought each other through the narrow passage out of hell that was Rebecca's mind: "as a…"

Then tears: Mildred's. "Oh for fuck," not even bothering to finish, allowing it, the cracked dam, the great flood. She only sat and looked at her lap and they both watched tear after tear hit her knees. As though she hadn't let this happen in decades. And now clumsy contrapuntal words wherever the sobs stopped long enough: "If you had met your uncle, Rebecca. If I, or we, he and I, had accepted how it's made, how it's done — the violence of that law against too much between two people."

"Mom."

"It's violent, sweetheart. It's *fucking*," voice cracking toward the sky, *"fucking, fucking, fucking violent.* It's so much *fucking* violence. God damn it!"

"Mom, please, relax."

"I can't relax, my baby. I can't. Twenty-six years."

"Twenty-six years."

"More or less."

"Since..."

"Yes. And the timing."

"The timing for what?"

"The timing, Becks, the, the, your father was in the," incapable, "the, your father was already there. It wasn't a teenage...fling. You're an adult, my love. I was an adult. McDurrrr was an adult. Your father was an adult."

"My father *what*, Mom?"

"He was there, in my life."

"Twenty-six years ago, this happened."

"It was the only chance. It felt like the one chance."

"To... be with..."

"With McDurrrr."

"But Dad was there."

"He was around. He loved me. Try, or don't, don't think too much, don't infer. Just let me."

"Let you tell me you fucked him? You," why was she saying this now, "fucked your brother? You fucked your brother, as an adult, while you were together with my *father*? This, this is what you," why so suddenly brutal, Rebecca, why make this harder, "you're saying you had an affair with Dad with your own brother?"

"Don't."

"Don't be cruel? Mother..."

"Don't."

"Mother, when was I..."

"Don't."

"You want me not to push? You want me to let you. Go ahead. Tell me," Rebecca's body now convulsing quietly, volcano-pumping, ejaculating what, earthquaking inside her little female human, young body, miscegenation by truth, "tell me, on," *I am going to carry this little nugget of awful truth in my head and you are fucking me with your honesty again yes, yes, yes, for once, not again, for the first time you're fucking me, mother*, "go on, go, tell me, say it as you want it said, go."

"Don't you dare!" Mildred's voice Stradivarius breaking against the wall, pieces, shards flying out, landing in your eyes: "Don't you talk to me like this. Ever, Rebecca. Don't spit at me when you *ask* for...when you come *back* for the things I decided not to share."

"Share? Your brother? Your two lovers? Whose — what am I, anyway?"

"Don't *attack* me, Rebecca. Don't destroy this. Please. Everything's so fucked already. I've kept so much from you, from Martha, from everyone. Your father. Myself. Please don't attack me. Please don't make me feel this death now. Not now."

"Okay."

"Just let me think."

"Okay."

"How to explain it, okay."

"Okay. Yes."

Mildred stood. She sat. "No, I have to get some water," and stood again.

"I'll get you some."

"The tap is a little tricky right now. You have to turn it right first."

"I'll figure it out."

"You have to push it to the right."

"Yeah, okay, I'll figure it out."

And Rebecca walked to the kitchen and opened a window

so the cigarette smell could, the cigarette smoke might leave. Leave us alone. Her hands now trembled now they trembled and the water. Focus your thinking on this. The water. The tap worked fine. She pushed it to the right and then pulled it up and the water flowed out. It smelled of chlorine. Like from childhood, when her hair used to stink of it. The pool. This smell of chlorine, always somewhere between disgusting and familiar, when I left the pool water rolling down the length of my legs crushing on the floor, I remember that smell of chlorine at least and the stream of water running past my thighs and knees and landing beneath my feet. Because I had to pee. And could not do it in the pool because of the others. Almost jogging back to the house and getting the seat wet as soon as I sat on it but at least I was grown up about things. And mother watching the others when I got back, making sure nobody was drowning. Even then I knew she couldn't relax, had to open her eyes and look at all the others in case one of them drowned. Because she would never forgive herself. A little swimming pool afternoon for me and the other kids but my mother was struck relaxing in stutters because she was terrified secretly that she'd be to blame for the death of a child. Even then: obvious — that connection, that bond we probably had but chalked up to whatever we could think of that was not familial love. But that was years later and mother was young and I was barely alive except by virtue of a few innocent years kept together by her care. Years had already passed since the, yes, this thing mother's trying to tell me — the incident is what she could call it. But it was not an incident. Such things don't happen so you can dismiss them with false names. The unacceptable yes. The forbidden bullshit nightmare. She might never have told me until it was almost irrelevant, so far into the past that it shocked me only because of the brutality of the secret. And I'm standing here while she waits for her waiting and I'm only thinking about that day by the pool when I was a child and I'm already led astray. I can focus on little memories but they are not there to help but to distract. The memories come from my mother. I remember through her. Because when I think back and remember my mother nervous and watching over my toddler friends and her toddler, little me, when I recall the dinners she made, always insisting on vegetables, and the days after the death of the father, maybe my father, if I could summon up a memory, all these memories amount to an epilogue. The action takes place so much earlier. "You want ice cubes?"

"They're in the freezer."

"I imagine they would be." Almost lighthearted now. Almost trivial. Mother would you like some ice cubes. Yes please they are in the freezer. What a convenient place to store them because that is where it is coldest in this house. Yes. She walked to the living room holding two cups of water with ice cubes that clinked with her steps. She sat. They drank. A pleasant summer silence.

"What happened with him? With McDurrrr?"

"It's not obvious to me, even," Mildred said. "It's a mess in here. In my head. When I think about that. It wasn't before, because I had to explain things to myself only. Now it's not so clear."

"You spent my lifetime thinking about all this. You raised me while you were thinking about it. Right? When I talked to you about myself, you must have been thinking about it. About me finding out. Right? About the day you would tell me."

"I wasn't going to tell you. For a long time it was none of your business, as far as I could make sense of it."

"And now you've told me. In part. That you and your brother were…um. You haven't confirmed it. Not enough. Do I want to know enough to ask you to confirm it?"

Mildred opened her mouth, weary, ready to respond, but everyone suddenly died. Haha.

**PERFECT
EDGE
BOOKS**

We live in uncertainty. New ways of committing crimes are discovered every day. Hackers and hit men are idolized. Writers have responded to this either by ignoring the harsher realities or by glorifying mindless violence for the sake of it. Atrocities (from the Holocaust to 9/11) are exploited in cheaply sentimental films and novels.

Perfect Edge Books proposes to find a balanced position. We publish fiction that doesn't revel in nihilism, doesn't go for gore at the cost of substance — yet we want to confront the world with its beauty as well as its ugliness. That means we want books about difficult topics, books with something to say.

We're open to dark comedies, "transgressive" novels, potboilers and tales of revenge. All we ask is that you don't try to shock for the sake of shocking — there is too much of that around. We are looking for intelligent young authors able to use the written word for changing how we read and write in dark times.